GIDEON'S
G LAW

Also Available from
STEIN AND DAY

GIDEON'S FORCE
William Vivian Butler
writing as
J.J. Marric

GIDEON'S
LAW

William Vivian Butler writing as

J.J. MARRIC

STEIN AND DAY/*Publishers*/New York

First published in the United States of America in 1986.
Copyright © 1981 by the executers of the late John Creasey
Published by arrangement with Harold Ober Associates
All rights reserved.
Printed in the United States of America.
Stein and Day, Incorporated
Scarborough House
Briarcliff Manor, N.Y. 10510

Library of Congress Cataloging-in-Publication Data

Butler, William Vivian, 1927-
  Gideon's law.

  I. Creasey, John.   II. Title.
PR6052.U875G55   1986   823'.914   85-40257
ISBN 0-8128-3042-3

To
MARY
with all my love
BILL

Contents

1 Trial

The noticeboard outside the No. 1 Court at the Old Bailey announced that the case being heard was that of the Crown versus Sidney Leon Vincent Stannet. But from the moment that the Defence Counsel, Sir Richard Ainley, rose to his feet, another man had really been on trial: Chief Detective Superintendent Thomas Riddell.

And they weren't trying only *him*, Riddell thought miserably, but by implication his chief, Commander Gideon, and the whole of the C.I.D.

Sidney Stannet was the most successful vice racketeer in London. Ainley was one of the cleverest, if most dubious, silks in the country. The two had been expected to make a formidable combination; but the defence they had put up had stunned the court, the jury – and the nation.

Carefully schooled and rehearsed witnesses had been produced from nowhere to swear blind that all the police evidence was faked. Riddell himself had been openly accused of planting "verbals" (false confessions); "leaning heavily on" (in other words, physically assaulting) suspects during interrogations; bribing at least three of the prosecution witnesses; threatening half-a-dozen others, and even forging incriminating documents.

A lot of these accusations had been self-evident perjuries. Others had been exposed as such through skilful cross-questioning by the Prosecuting Counsel. But with so much expertly-processed mud flying about, some was bound to stick.

To anyone who knew Tom Riddell, of course, *all* the charges were ludicrous. Although he had his faults as a policeman – obstinacy, aggressiveness and a nervous tension that had several times brought him to the edge of a breakdown – there was no one more honest in the whole of the Metropolitan Police Force. But it wasn't honesty that counted in a no-holds-barred trial like this. It was the ability to look completely self-assured. Only that could have out-faced the fake defence witnesses. Only that could have beaten the polished Sir Richard Ainley at his own game.

There were plenty of his colleagues at the Yard who *could* have put on such a performance, Riddell knew. He went through their names enviously in his mind. There was George Gideon himself, for instance. One genuine Gideon roar and Ainley would have been shaking in his immaculately-polished shoes. Then there was Alec Hobbs, Gideon's deputy. Just a touch of Alec's imperturbable suavity would have changed the whole atmosphere in the courtroom – and kept the image of the police force where it ought to be, and where in this case it *deserved* to be: totally above suspicion.

Whereas he, Riddell realised bitterly, had done completely the opposite. The very thought of the performance he had put up made his temples throb and his armpits sweat.

How *could* an officer of his experience – thirty years in the force, twenty of them as Chief Detective Superintendent – have made such a poor showing in the witness-box? He had given evidence on hundreds – no, thousands – of occasions, always efficiently, sometimes extremely effectively.

Riddell knew that he had it in him to impress. A large man, brown-eyed, brown-haired, he had once been massive and almost commanding. But the years had thinned him, both outwardly and inwardly. There were moments now when his body looked gaunt, his eyes haunted, his whole appearance haggard: and there had been far too many such moments during the five hours that Ainley had kept him under relentless, almost jeering, cross-examination.

"I put it to you, Chief Detective Superintendent, that

everything you have said since you stepped into the witness-box has been a tissue of lies."

The words, although they had been uttered a good half-hour before, still echoed and re-echoed round Riddell's head, each repetition seeming to send a fresh shock wave coursing through his nerves.

He had not, in fact, told a single, solitary half-truth from that witness-box, let alone a tissue of lies.

That fact should have been self-evident from his face, from his bearing, from his manner. Had Gideon or Hobbs been in his place, the charge would have seemed so ludicrous that there would probably have been laughter in court.

Yes. *Laughter.*

Not that stunned, strained silence, during which all eyes, even the judge's, seemed to be turned on him accusingly – and, worst of all, during which the whole courtroom had seemed to whirl round . . .

He had actually had to fight to stop himself swaying. Just in time, he had remembered to keep his hands clasped firmly behind his back. Nothing betrayed guilt so much as a hand clutching the sides of a witness-box, knuckles whitening over the ledge. He had beaten the dizziness the old parade-ground way: shuffling his feet imperceptibly, and taking a long, deep breath.

By the time he had taken it, the moment had passed. Ainley, with a contemptuous shrug and an "I-told-you-so" smile, had murmured, "Your witness" to the Prosecution and returned to his seat. The Prosecuting Counsel, after a shrewd look in the Yard man's direction, had decided not to prolong Riddell's ordeal, and simply responded: "No further questions."

Riddell, shakily, had returned to his seat, a special bench reserved for witnesses at the back of the court; and the Prosecution had begun its summing-up.

It was a summing-up that was still going on.

Riddell found it painful to listen to.

All the evidence he had spent weeks and months amassing against the Stannet vice ring ("a watertight case, if ever I've seen one, Tom," Gideon had said) now seemed flimsy in the extreme.

11

No wonder, Riddell thought savagely.

The strongest case in the world would be bound to look threadbare once the suspicion had been aroused in the jury's mind that the police were intimidating witnesses, and extracting confessions under duress. And today those suspicions had not only been aroused, but confirmed, minute by minute, by his weakness in the box. Five hours – five solid hours – he'd given them of anxious looks and hesitant replies. All right, so he'd stopped himself swaying at the culmination of it all. But if he'd keeled over like a ninepin, it couldn't have made the situation any worse.

The case was lost. Stannet had won hands down, and from the look of him, already knew it.

The acknowledged vice king of London – a pink-faced, balding man whom not even a Savile Row suit could save from looking grossly overweight – was lounging in the dock as comfortably as if he was leaning against the counter of a saloon bar. He was not very far from actually smirking.

"You wait, my friend," Riddell found himself muttering. But then his anger faded, to be replaced by a baffled sense of helplessness. If watertight evidence could be scuttled by the simple expedient of spending the right money in the right places to make the police look suspect, then how could justice ever win against the Stannets of this world?

Meanwhile, one thing was certain. And at the thought of it, Riddell's head throbbed so painfully that it felt as though his forehead was caving in.

Nothing could now stop the jury from finding Sid Stannet "Not Guilty" . . . and by the same token, passing unmistakable judgment on Gideon's C.I.D. and all that it stood for.

Riddell wondered miserably what Gideon would think.

And if he would ever forgive him.

2 Confrontation

At that precise moment, George Gideon was having almost as
agonising a time as Tom Riddell; and once again, it was the
Stannet case that was responsible.

Sir Reginald Scott-Marle, the Commissioner, had summoned
him to his office; and the moment he entered the room, Gideon
knew why. Scott-Marle's desk was covered with newpapers, all
of them headlining the Old Bailey trial.

"SENIOR   YARD   MAN   BRIBED   WITNESSES,
DEFENCE ALLEGES."
" 'GESTAPO' METHODS USED BY C.I.D., SAYS
COUNSEL."
" 'FAKED CONFESSIONS FRAMED MY CLIENT'
ACCUSES TOP Q.C."
" 'C.I.D.   FRAMED   DOCUMENTS   WHOLESALE,'
COURT TOLD . . ."

The headlines were familiar to Gideon. They had been staring
up at him from his own desk earlier that morning – until, in
a moment of extreme exasperation, he had screwed them up and
swept them into the wastepaper bin. Not that that had changed
anything, he reflected ruefully. The British public wouldn't be
tearing up any of these papers. In millions of homes, they'd be
gleefully lapping up the scandalous assertions. And believing
them. That was the thought that hurt. A great many years' work

13

building up the prestige of the Force had been destroyed in a few short hours – just by one unscrupulous barrister's performance, and one clever criminal's money.

Scott-Marle glanced up, saw Gideon's grim look and needed no telling that all this hurt the C.I.D.'s Commander as deeply as it hurt him.

"Sit down, George," he said, almost gently, and indicated a chair. Gideon did not walk across to it: he *strode*, his massive frame looking as if it would bulldoze anything or anyone in his way. But that fierce progress was the only sign he gave of the anger and frustration he was feeling. As he sat – easing himself surprisingly effortlessly into the chair for so big a man – he actually managed to grin.

"Well, we've had the book thrown at us often enough before," he said. "Even if this time it feels like all the volumes of the Encyclopaedia Britannica coming at once."

Scott-Marle smiled very faintly. Otherwise his face was quite expressionless. He was a quiet, remote man whom Gideon had once thought cold. Long experience, though, had taught him that Scott-Marle's dedication to the Force was, in its own way, as intense as his own.

"You're still sure that we're in a position to refute all these charges?" he asked suddenly.

"More than a dozen counter-charges of perjury are on their way to the Public Prosecutor's Office today," Gideon said. "It is, of course, Stannet and Ainley who've been forging documents, bribing and intimidating witnesses, and pretty certainly using Gestapo methods as well. The trouble is, it'll take weeks of work to winkle out all the facts – and the jury's verdict is expected tomorrow. If, as I suspect, it turns out to be 'Not Guilty' – "

"The public will pass a 'Guilty' verdict on *us*," said Scott-Marle. "And in particular, on Riddell." His tone suddenly changed, and became sharper. "George. It's about Riddell that I want to talk to you."

Gideon took a deep breath. He didn't like the sound of this. A mental image of Tom's face – now so often haggard and

14

haunted – flashed in front of his eyes. If Scott-Marle was going to suggest using him as any sort of a scapegoat . . .

"There isn't an officer in the C.I.D. with a finer record," he said, almost belligerently. "Only a few years ago, he was recommended for the George Medal, for saving the lives of a family of immigrants when the house they were living in collapsed on top of them."

"His courage isn't in dispute," Scott-Marle conceded blandly. "Though I *could* wish he'd displayed a little more of it in court. He suffers from nervous tension, I see from the files." The Commissioner looked up, and the expression in his eyes made Gideon remember why for so long he had thought him cold. "To be brutally frank, George, had you considered the possibility that Riddell's trouble might have escalated, without you realising it? On the brink of a breakdown, even the most responsible officer may do things which – he later regrets."

Only with iron self-control did Gideon prevent himself from leaping up from his chair, and crashing his fist down on the Commissioner's desk.

As it was, he simply couldn't keep the anger out of his voice as he said: "You're suggesting that, for all we know, some of the charges against Riddell might be true?"

Scott-Marle was now at his blandest.

"I'm suggesting that it's a matter for an inquiry, yes," he said. "In fairness to Riddell himself, as much as anyone else. It would only be a question of suspending him for a few weeks, and getting A10 to verify his statements."

A10 was Scotland Yard's new self-investigating unit. It was staffed by ordinary policemen, some from Uniform and some from the C.I.D., who were taken off their normal duties for two years, and required to spend that time inquiring into complaints about their fellow officers. A10 work was the most loathed and dreaded job that came a Yard man's way. It often meant cross-questioning old colleagues, and sometimes came close to spying on old friends. But no one was allowed to refuse A10 duty; and most carried it out faithfully and well.

Although many of the complaints A10 investigated turned out

to be quite unfounded, most were not. If Tom was suspended from duty, and it became known that A10 were investigating him, he would be living under a stigma for the rest of his career.

Gideon suddenly *was* standing; and although he did not bang on the Commissioner's desk, he towered over it, which was almost as startling.

Quietly – impressively quietly – he said: "*Only* a question of suspending him? Believe me, if we put Tom through an ordeal like that, straight on top of what he's been enduring at this trial, we will utterly destroy him! Surely that's a very poor reward for thirty years of good, and sometimes outstanding, service, to say nothing of the brilliant work he's put in on this very case! For close on a year, he's been slogging for seventeen or eighteen hours a day, building up what, under ordinary circumstances, would have been a *cast-iron* case against Stannet."

Gideon's voice rose.

"If the consequences of working like a dog, and achieving such results, are to be suspension and disgrace, then I do not see how I could honestly encourage anyone in the C.I.D. to take on racketeers like Stannet in future."

Gideon's voice rose again, until – although he did not realise it – he was actually subjecting Scott-Marle to the full Gideon roar.

"And in a situation where the C.I.D. is helpless against anyone rich enough to engage unscrupulous counsels, and bribe or bully sufficient lying witnesses – *then I would have no wish to remain its Commander.*"

There was a long, long silence while Gideon and the Commissioner stared at each other. Their faces were barely eighteen inches apart. It was almost literally an eyeball-to-eyeball confrontation.

Scott-Marle's face remained totally expressionless. Only the fact that for a good three seconds it was completely frozen – not an eyelid blinking, not a muscle twitching – suggested that behind the façade, Scott-Marle might actually be shaken.

Gideon tried to keep his own face impassive, but he doubted if he was succeeding. He only hoped that it didn't betray too much

16

of the conflicting emotions seething inside him.

On a few – a very few – previous occasions in his long and complex relationship with Scott-Marle, he had come close to resigning. But he had never in the past gone further than to hint at the possibility: and had seldom done that without carefully thinking it over first, and consulting with his wife, Kate, about what it would mean to both of them. This time, though, without the slightest premeditation, he had been reckless enough to deliver what must have sounded like an ultimatum, if not an outright declaration of war.

Oh, well, it was too late now. He had burnt his boats with a vengeance – a whole fleetful of them. And strangely enough, fundamentally, he had no regrets. Because what he had roared at Scott-Marle, with such passionate intensity that it felt as though a long-sleeping volcano had erupted inside him, was nothing more or less than the truth. If the Commissioner was not going to support his men when, through no fault of their own, they got a bad public image, then in all honesty and honour, he could no longer stay at the Yard. It was as simple as that. And neither Kate nor anyone else could have expected him to act in any other way.

Sir Reginald moved at last. He leant back in his chair, and was suddenly faintly – very, very faintly – smiling.

"Take it easy, George. If the situation were really what you've described, I would be ahead of you in the resignation queue. Sit down again, for Heaven's sake, and let's talk this over calmly."

Gideon returned awkwardly to his chair, feeling confused and discomforted by Scott-Marle's impenetrable smoothness.

"I should make one thing very clear," the Commissioner proceeded. "If Riddell is as clean as a whistle in all this, as you suggest, then of course everyone at Scotland Yard will back him to a man."

"By suspending him the moment he returns to his office?" Gideon growled. "Forgive me, but I don't see how that can be called 'backing him'. It comes closer to *stabbing* him in the back!"

Scott-Marle thought for a moment, and then, to Gideon's

astonishment and relief, relented.

"Point taken, George. All right: there will be no suspension."

"And no A10 investigation?"

"None that anyone but him need know about."

Gideon leant forward, frowning.

"Meaning?"

"Meaning that A10 will have to be called in, but will be under orders to be extemely discreet. They will question Riddell only at his home, after hours. And when questioning anybody else, they will leave Riddell's name right out of it, and make it seem that they are conducting purely general inquiries into the C.I.D." For once, Scott-Marle's smile was almost broad. "Will that do? You can't say I haven't gone a long way towards meeting you."

Gideon did not return the smile.

"Frankly, what I still can't understand," he said, "is why there has to be an inquiry at all."

For answer, Scott-Marle gestured towards the newspapers.

"You and I have gone through these with a toothcomb," he said. "Do you imagine the Home Office won't be doing the same? The moment that jury returns a 'Not Guilty' verdict, I shall have the Home Secretary on the phone, demanding a report. And he will simply not be satisfied with a report that relies on C.I.D. evidence alone. To keep him happy, I'll have to bring in A10 too. They represent Uniform as well as the C.I.D., and have a reputation for impartiality."

"Which I haven't?" said Gideon sourly.

"To be honest, George, where your own men are concerned, no." Scott-Marle picked up a copy of *The Times*. "Take this witness's story here. 'Chief Detective Superintendent Riddell hit me so that the back of my head struck the wall three times. "Sign this," he shouted, "or you'll get more of the same – ten times more of it." ' Now you, knowing Riddell as you do, would dismiss that out of hand."

"Not if an honest witness had said it," Gideon snapped.

"But how can you be sure that some of Stannet's witnesses *weren't* honest? Riddell has made a pretty poor showing against them in court."

18

Gideon took a deep breath.

"May I point out that Riddell is not on trial," he said, adding bitterly: "Perhaps it would be better if he were. At least he'd be innocent then until proved guilty."

At last, Scott-Marle showed slight signs of emotion. Almost heatedly, he said: "I can assure you, that is the position now. As far as I am concerned, he is innocent until his guilt is proved up to the hilt. And I am as confident as you are that it never will be. On that basis will you agree to this inquiry?"

Gideon saw that there was no way in which he could refuse. If he held out any further, Scott-Marle would be bound to suspect that both he – and the C.I.D. – had something to hide.

Slowly, he stood up.

"Very reluctantly," he said, "I do."

"Fine," said Scott-Marle briskly. His face was expressionless again, his tone as casual as if there had never been any question of a rift between them. "And let's hope for all our sakes that Stannet is found guilty. Then none of this unpleasantness need arise. Once a defence collapses, it collapses, and none of its witnesses are taken seriously. Well, I don't think there's anything else we need discuss, just for the moment, is there? I have a conference in a few minutes – "

He was dismissing Gideon as plainly as if he had gone to the door and opened it.

Gideon obediently left the room, walking with something less than his usual purposeful stride.

It had been a titanic battle, but he was not sure if he had won or lost the day.

On the one hand, he had saved Riddell from suspension, and the stigma of a full-scale A10 investigation.

On the other hand, he had agreed to Riddell being forced to undergo the totally undeserved humiliation of prying colleagues calling at his home.

Gideon wondered miserably what Riddell would think.

And if *he* would ever forgive *him*.

3 The Questioners

There had been a very few periods in Gideon's life when he had been able to devote his whole time to one problem; and this was certainly not one of them.

Whatever battles he might have fought or won, however anxious he might be about Riddell, the Stannet case and public confidence in the Force, there was still a day of running the C.I.D. to be faced.

That meant a deskload of work to be ploughed through; upwards of a score of investigations to be supervised, some from a distance, some in detail, and countless tricky decisions to be taken, as a result of which fresh inquiries would be initiated, stale ones revitalised, promising ones extended and dead-end ones abandoned. They were decisions that Gideon had learned to make quickly, but could never bring himself to take casually. Upon them – as no one knew better than he – depended the whole thrust, drive and tempo of London's non-stop fight against crime.

As days went, this looked as if it was going to be a tough one. A light November drizzle was streaming over London, but there was nothing light about the shower of appointments landing on his desk.

The moment he arrived back in his office, he found his deputy Alec Hobbs, writing a couple more of them on his note-pad.

"All right, tell me the worst," he said, with an attempt at a grin. "Who are you press-ganging me into seeing now?"

"Farrant at eleven forty-five, Honiwell at twelve fifteen," Hobbs said. "If that's all right with you."

Gideon started.

"Farrant! That'll be the Dante case. Has there been an important development there?"

It would be a great relief if there had.

"Dante" was the soubriquet used by an arsonist of a new and extremely dangerous kind: a maniac who specialised in creating flamboyant and spectacular blazes, usually by setting light to paint factories or chemical warehouses. He had left a trail of fifteen such fires in three months, usually around South London industrial estates. Six of the fires – the ones in paint factories – had set off series of explosions. Others had created potentially lethal gas clouds, and the areas involved had had to be evacuated.

Three firemen killed; seventeen others seriously injured; a night watchman with a leg blown off; a passer-by who had lost an eye – that was the grim toll that this maniac had already left behind him. And yet he seemed to take a flamboyant pride in his work. After every crime in the series, the same two words had been found chalked on a nearby door, gate or wall:

DANTE'S INFERNO

This suggested a man with some literary knowledge, and therefore possibly a higher-than-average education: but that was pure speculation. Up to the moment, a great deal about Dante had been pure speculation, including the agonising hours Gideon had spent wondering where and when he might strike next. The trouble with a spectacular blaze was that it almost automatically removed all traces of the perpetrator. What clue could survive in the heart of a holocaust of blazing chemicals or exploding paint?

But it seemed as if something had turned up now – at last.

"A *very* important development, I think," Hobbs was saying, in answer to Gideon's question. "Farrant was downright cock-a-hoop on the phone just now."

"Farrant is *always* downright cock-a-hoop," said Gideon heavily. "Didn't he tell you anything specific?"

"Oh, yes. He's charged someone with being Dante and got

21

him to Down Lane station for questioning. That's a new police station on an industrial estate near Morden."

Gideon whistled.

"If Farrant has the slightest shred of evidence to back that up, then this *is* good news."

Hobbs smiled.

"You're always a Doubting Thomas where Farrant is concerned."

"A *cautious* Thomas, certainly," Gideon said.

John Farrant was the newest – and youngest – Chief Detective Superintendent in the Metropolitan C.I.D. He had a long list of successful investigations to his credit, as a result of which he had shot up like a rocket in the Department; but Gideon could never escape the feeling that he had progressed suspiciously fast. There was nothing he could pin down, and Gideon disliked himself for harbouring an irrational suspicion of anybody, least of all someone so able and enthusiastic. He could only hope that his sixth sense – that uncanny knack he had of sizing a man up on sight, and rarely estimating him wrongly – had, for once, failed him.

Gideon sank down heavily behind his desk, and considered Hobbs's second note.

"Did Honiwell say what he wanted to see me about?"

"Yes. He's also taken a man in for questioning, in this case at Aldgate. A garage owner called Lenny Haig."

"Is this to do with that bank snatch in Blackfriars Street yesterday? If so, it's very quick work."

"Yes. Honiwell had a lucky break. Lenny Haig was careless, and left his thumbprint on the steering-wheel of the abandoned getaway car. Records had no trouble identifying it, because he did a stretch some years ago for receiving stolen cars."

"H'm," said Gideon. "Pity we've only caught the getaway driver. It's the brains behind the bloody gang we want. And I'm not using 'bloody' as a swearword."

The Blackfriars snatch had, in fact, been the most murderous incident of its kind that year. The gang had had sawn-off shotguns and revolvers, and had become hysterically trigger-

22

happy with both. A security man had been hit in the head; a girl bank clerk in the stomach, and the bank manager in the lung. The gang had got clean away with £300,000. If, thought Gideon angrily, one could call anything clean that left such a mass of death and writhing agony behind it . . .

He wondered what the chances were of this Lenny Haig turning informer on the rest of the mob. He feared that they were probably slim. Getaway drivers were a close-mouthed lot, far too scared of their leaders to do much squealing as a rule. And with a lethal mob like this at his back, Haig was unlikely to prove an exception.

Still, if anyone could get information out of him, it was Honiwell. There was no one at the Yard with such a sympathetic way with people – criminals and victims alike – than the mild, almost cuddly-looking Matt.

Gideon glanced up, and saw that Hobbs was still hovering, almost awkwardly, in the doorway. He stared. It was very unlike Alec to hover – or, indeed, to do anything awkwardly at all.

Suave, immaculate, nearly always calm and composed, Alec had a lot in common with Scott-Marle – except that he lacked Scott-Marle's remoteness.

These days, Alec needed all his composure. He was walking a difficult, almost impossible tightrope professionally. Officially, he was still functioning as Gideon's deputy – and making a superb job of it, taking more and more of the run-of-the-mill decisions out of Gideon's hands. But the post of Assistant Commissioner (Crime) had been vacant for a long time now, and it was common knowledge that Alec would almost certainly be appointed to it. In other words, at any moment he might change from being Gideon's assistant to his superior!

Gideon was not in the least disturbed about this situation. In fact, he had engineered it. Scott-Marle had repeatedly invited Gideon himself to be the new A.C., but after months of deep reflection, Gideon had decided that he was too near retirement age to tackle it. In any case, he had argued, he was first and foremost a policeman, not a boardroom-level administrator. He had therefore recommended Alec for the post, and was more than pleased that he was now so close to getting it – for personal as well as professional reasons. About a year earlier, Alec had married Gideon's youngest daughter Penny. It had seemed, to outward appearances, an unlikely match: Alec was a widower in his middle forties and a dedicated policeman; Penny was in her middle twenties and passionately involved with a musical career. She was, in fact, a highly-praised concert pianist. Yet despite these differences in their ages, their interests and their careers, Gideon had never known a happier couple; and they seemed to be happier still with every month that passed.

He suddenly guessed the reason for Alex's momentary hovering. Obviously he was going to mention something personal, and even after a year of marriage, found it hard to make the transition from Deputy Commander to son-in-law.

Gideon decided to help him out.

"A message from Penny?" he asked, blandly.

Alec's instant smile showed that his guess had hit the mark.

"Er – from both of us," he said. "Penny and I have got the house pretty well straight now."

This was the new house near Hurlingham which they'd moved into a couple of months before. Although it was only a mile from Gideon's front door, Penny had begged her parents not even to drive past it, until it was spick and span, and Gideon and Kate had sternly resisted the temptation to do so.

"We were wondering if you and Kate were free to come over this evening, for a bit of a house-warming," Alec went on. "Sorry it's such short notice, but we were waiting for a new dining-room suite, which only arrived yesterday. And the party has to be tonight. Penny's got concert rehearsals every evening for the rest of the week."

"Don't worry. I know all about Penny's rehearsals," Gideon said, half ruefully, half nostalgically. "They've played havoc with all our domestic arrangements for years."

"Do you think you and Kate can come?"

Gideon grinned broadly.

"I'll have to ring Kate and ask her, of course. But I think I can tell you the answer. Just try and keep us away!"

Alec returned Gideon's grin with a debonaire smile, and was about to go. Then he swung round, his fingers still on the handle of the door.

"Oh, George ..." Suddenly he wasn't smiling. "There's one piece of news which I think I ought to pass on. The story's going round that Tom Riddell nearly passed out at the Old Bailey this morning. And he picked the worst possible moment to do it. When the Defence Counsel had just suggested that everything he'd been saying was a tissue of lies."

"Oh, God!" Gideon groaned. "That's torn it. It'll seem to the whole country like a straight admission of guilt. As if Tom wasn't in enough trouble already ..."

He told Hobbs about the A10 inquiry.

There was a pause, during which Alec's face became as expressionless as Scott-Marle's. For a long moment, Gideon wondered if he was going to say that he agreed that an inquiry was necessary.

Quite the opposite turned out to be the case. The normally restrained Hobbs suddenly gave vent to an outburst of indignation that nearly rocked the room.

"It's one thing to turn A10 on to men about whom we've got serious doubts. But to start an A10 inquiry on someone who's so obviously been framed ... why, it's — it's diabolical. Almost like playing into the enemy's hands. What the hell does Scott-Marle think he's doing?"

The strength of the attack, and the note of authority behind it, astonished Gideon, and for a moment almost shocked him. Then, suddenly, he chuckled.

It wasn't surprising he was bewildered. In the space of a few short minutes, he'd been listening to three entirely different Alec Hobbses.

His Deputy Commander. His son-in-law. And the future Assistant Commissioner (Crime).

With a warm glow spreading inside him, Gideon decided that he liked the sound of all three.

*   *   *

The last of Gideon's warm feeling faded about ten minutes later, when Chief Detective Superintendent John Farrant entered the room.

Farrant, still in his middle thirties, was darkly good-looking, with black crinkly hair, keen grey eyes – and such sharp features that his face always reminded Gideon of the old joke about two profiles stuck together. Everything about him registered energy, drive and an insatiable hunger to get on. That partly explained his quick promotion, of course. He combined the sort of personality that gets noticed with the kind of looks that get remembered.

Altogether, a highly impressive young man: and Gideon wondered again why something inside him refused to let him be impressed.

Farrant's opening remark was typical.

"I see you have the file on the Dante case there, sir. Well, I've good news for you. You can virtually consider it closed."

Others might have been amused by such effrontery. Gideon was not.

He very deliberately opened the file, and spread out its contents. There were so many papers in it that they covered almost the whole of his desk.

"This file will not be closed, Farrant, until a great many things have happened," he barked. "Until Dante, whoever he may be, has been positively identified on unimpeachable evidence – *and* been found guilty in a court of law. If you take my advice, you'll stop crowing until you've achieved all that. And since you're dealing with the most cunning and elusive arsonist of the decade, I doubt if you're anywhere near achieving it yet. I understand that you've charged a man and taken him in for questioning. 1 am waiting – and hoping – to hear that you had solid grounds for doing so. If you have, I'll be the first to congratulate you." He paused, then added heavily: "If I can be heard above the sound of you congratulating yourself."

Even as he finished speaking, Gideon wondered if he had gone too far. It had been a brutally withering attack, and would have flattened almost any other man in the C.I.D.

But Farrant did not even seem taken aback. He was, if anything, more cocksure than ever.

"Perhaps I'd better let the facts speak for themselves, sir. I think they'll do so clearly enough. The man I arrested is an alcoholic vagrant, who —"

"An alcoholic vagrant? And you believe *he* could be Dante?"

"I think there are very strong indications that point that way, sir, yes."

"Then I can tell you three things straight off that point in the opposite direction. Dante is a very skilful, sophisticated operator. He knows how to start exactly the right kind of fire at precisely the most vulnerable points of factories and warehouses that are carefully chosen for their combustability. He must have an expert knowledge of chemistry, a keen analytical mind, a very sharp pair of eyes and exceptionally steady hands. Does any of that suggest an alcoholic, still less a vagrant?"

Farrant still did not flinch.

"This particular vagrant, yes, sir. He's only recently become a 'drop-out'. Less than a year ago, he was a senior research chemist at Nitro Power, a firm specialising in explosives for dam constructors and the like."

Gideon whistled softly. That, he had to admit, made a difference.

"He left Nitro Power last January," Farrant continued, "after a nervous breakdown, and spent the next six months in a mental hospital, from which he was discharged last August 6th, ten days before the first of the Dante fires, on August 16th, at Wimbledon. He admits to having lived in the South London area — constantly changing his quarters, but mostly lodging in doss houses and squatters' communes — during the whole of the last three months. Which means he has always been near the big South London industrial estates, scene of all the Dante crimes. And three times during the past four days, he's been seen hanging suspiciously around the Mortimer Paint Factory at Morden, which is almost certainly intended to be his next target."

It was Gideon, now, who was taken aback. He had to admit that Farrant was building up a strong case ... even if a purely circumstantial one.

"It was the Mortimer's Paint people who put you on to him?"

"That's it, sir. The man at the gate reported him to the police at Down Lane, and they in turn got on to me. I sent two men down to watch him, and put the rest of my men on to digging up all these facts about him."

"Didn't these facts include a name?" snapped Gideon. "Do we have to keep talking about him as though he was completely anonymous?"

Farrant smiled. It was a tight, arrow-shaped smile, the broadest his sharp features would allow.

"They certainly did find out his name. In fact, it was that which first convinced me that he merited further investigation. It's Timothy Dane, sir. And he usually signs himself *T. Dane* — a complete anagram of *'Dante'.*"

Gideon slowly stood up.

"Well, Farrant, I said congratulations would be in order if you made out a reasonable case, and this certainly comes under that heading. You've also done some first-class work to come up with all this so fast. Would you like a drink?"

He fetched a bottle of whisky, two glasses and a soda syphon out of a cubby-hole in the corner. It was a little early for drinking, but after the way he'd treated Farrant when he first came in, he didn't feel it was any too soon to make amends.

"I don't withdraw all my objections, though," he said, as soon as the drinks were finished and put away. "The evidence is still basically circumstantial, and even the name anagram *could* be a coincidence. In your place, I think I'd have held off making an arrest, and set a trap at Mortimer Paints. Then you might have caught him red-handed — and *really* closed the case! As it is, all we can hope is that something more emerges when you get down to questioning Dane."

An odd, almost sly look came over Farrant's face; his smile levelled into a thin, cruel line.

"Don't you worry, sir," he said softly. "A great deal more *will* emerge, I promise you, before I've done with him."

Gideon glowered.

"I never thought the day would come when I'd have to give this warning to any member of my staff," he said. "But just in case you're tempted, Farrant, remember this: I will have no mercy on any officer who doesn't keep his interrogation methods absolutely clean. Have I made myself clear?"

Farrant, as usual, was not in the least non-plussed.

"Perfectly," he said, as perfunctorily as though he was complying to a meaningless ritual. In much the same tone, he added: "I'll be on my way to Down Lane then. I'll keep you in touch, sir. And thanks for the drink."

A second later, he was gone, leaving Gideon staring after him, all his suspicions returning with redoubled force.

*   *   *

It was a great relief when, a couple of minutes later, Matt Honiwell came in to discuss the Blackfriars Street snatch case.

There was no friendlier, more human person in the C.I.D. than Matt. Though many criminals had learnt to their cost that he wasn't quite as soft as his "cuddly" appearance suggested, he had a genuinely sympathetic nature, and excelled on cases where human problems needed tactful handling. His only fault as a policeman was that he tended to become too deeply involved with those problems, and to make other people's worries his own.

He was already feeling slightly guilty about the garage-owner-cum-getaway-driver whom he'd arrested, Lenny Haig.

"I had to call at his house and drag him from the bosom of his family. Wife sobbing, children screaming – Christ, I'll never get used to that side of our business, never in a thousand years."

"Does he have a lot of children?"

"Six – all ages from a girl of about twelve to three boys who looked eighteen-to-twenty. It was the girl who was doing the screaming, of course ..."

"Never mind that," said Gideon grimly. "Think about the other screaming that was going on yesterday. That girl bank clerk hit in the stomach ... the bank manager hit in a lung. That'll make you feel a bit less sympathetic towards this Lenny

29

Haig." He paused, a thought striking him. "How are the victims, by the way?"

"Both reported as being reasonably comfortable," Matt said. "Although with the girl, it's been a touch-and-go night. The security man who was hit in the head, though—he died this morning, without recovering consciousness. Oh, it's a bad business, no one's denying that, though whether Lenny had all that much to do with it is hard to say."

"Did he deny the charge?"

"Oh, no. He couldn't, really, in the face of that crystal-clear thumbprint he'd left on the steering-wheel. He had a most unusual defence, though. He claimed the gang *compelled* him to drive for them. Two men in stocking masks held his wife and family hostages at gunpoint from the time he left to the time he returned. He didn't report it to the police because, with his record, he thought he'd never be believed."

"Well, at least, that's original," Gideon said. "How about the family? Did they support the story?"

"They certainly did," said Matt. "Pretty convincingly, as a matter of fact. That twelve-year-old girl started to shake all over at the memory. Either the whole thing was an elaborate pre-arranged plot by the gang to provide their getaway man with a good alibi, just on the offchance he'd be pulled in—"

"Which seems, on the face of it, unlikely," mused Gideon.

"—or Lenny Haig is virtually innocent," concluded Matt. "In which case, we may be up against a blank wall. He may not know anything about the gang at all, except that they happened to pick him to drive for them."

"He'll find it tough to explain why they happened to do that, though."

"Not necessarily. Lenny's pretty well-known round the East End and he was once a professional racing driver. If the snatch had ended in a car-chase, he'd have been an ideal man to have behind the wheel."

Gideon sighed.

"I don't know whether you realise it, Matt, but you're almost coming in on his side."

30

Honiwell looked embarrassed.

"I admit, I can't help liking the man," he said. "*And* his family, for that matter. They're cheerful old-style Cockneys. Probably mixed up with all kinds of small-time shadiness. Everything in the house looked as if it had dropped off the back of a lorry, as they'd put it. But I simply can't see any of them taking part in a bloodbath. Lenny seemed really shaken up at the memory of it, and I don't think he's acting. As a matter of fact, he was in such a state that I had to stop questioning him. I'm giving him a couple of hours' rest. Then I'll be back to have another go at him this afternoon. If he looks as though he could stand it ... Have I said something wrong, George?"

Matt broke off, puzzled by the look on his superior's face.

"On the contrary," Gideon said softly, "you've said everything right. It's just such a relief to hear such a sane, normal and human attitude to questioning. It's probably the most vital job we do, but it's far and away the most thankless."

" 'Thankless' just about sums it up," said Matt. "Look at this bloody Stannet business. Tom's one of the best and straightest coppers that ever breathed, and yet – "

He ran a hand through his mop of brown, curly hair, still thick but now very noticeably streaked with grey. His voice was suddenly bitter and strained.

" – and yet I learned from Lenny this morning that the Underworld's just coined a new phrase for brutal and sadistic police behaviour. All over London – probably all over England by now – they're calling it 'doing a Riddell'."

31

4 The Questioned

For two hours, in the brightly-painted interrogation room at the new police station at Down Lane, Chief Detective Superintendent Farrant had – in the latest Underworld jargon – been "doing a Riddell" on Timothy Dane.

During that time, the grey and drizzly November afternoon had darkened into a bleak and gusty November night. This suited Farrant's purposes perfectly. All he had to do was time his blows with the frequent gusts of wind, and not a sound could be heard outside the smart green walls of the interrogation room.

There was no real risk in what he was doing, Farrant told himself. The man he was questioning so brutally might have an educated voice and manner, but he was still basically a doss-house alcoholic, the lowest of the low. Nothing he said would be believed, or taken much notice of, by anyone. You only had to take one look at him to see that. Dane was probably about the same age as Farrant, but looked twenty years older. His long – almost shoulder-length – black hair was greasy and unwashed. The lower half of his face was entirely hidden by a matted beard. The few inches of his skin that could be seen were grey with dirt. And his eyes – red-rimmed, watery and continually blinking – were blank and crazed.

He had been too stupid even to ask for a lawyer after he had been charged. The police social worker had sent for one on his behalf, an Indian called Darabji Singh who had made a perfunctory visit lasting four minutes, taken down the basic details of the charge, and gone his way.

"Don't imagine he's going to be much help to you, Dane," Farrant shouted. "Or that anyone else is, for that matter. You only have two choices. To tell the truth or have it beaten out of you, inch by bloody inch. ... Let's go back to the beginning, shall we? You've admitted – or half-admitted – that you are fascinated by fires ..."

"No, that's wrong. That's completely wrong." In insanely striking contrast to his rough appearance, Dane had a thin, piping voice, and spoke with the precision of a pedant. "I did not say that I was fascinated by fires. I said that I cannot escape from them. They follow me wherever I go. Every few weeks, I find them flaring, blazing, bursting round me."

Farrant seized him by the lapels of his filthy suit – a good suit, it had been, once; it was double-breasted and made of the finest worsted. Then he shook him violently to and fro, six or seven times. This was pathetically easy to do: the man was so thin and emaciated he couldn't have weighed more than five or six stone.

"It's hardly surprising that fires follow you, is it, chummy? Because you're crazy about them. Because you need them. Because they answer some perverted craving in your sick, twisted mind. In other words – because you're DANTE."

The watery eyes blinked. The thin voice quavered.

"I do wish you would not keep repeating that name. It means nothing to me, unless you are referring to the classical Italian poet – "

"Ah. You've heard of *him*, then."

"Of course."

"And his most famous book?"

"You may mean the *Divine Comedy*. You may mean its best-known part, the *Inferno* ..." Dane was suddenly shaking *himself* to and fro, in an attack of uncontrollable shivering. "The *Inferno* ... Fire again. Oh, God, can't I ever escape from *fire*?"

"You certainly can," said Farrant heavily. "Just sign this bit of paper and we'll keep you locked away from it for years."

33

Still shaking, Dane backed away against a wall.

"I have told you repeatedly that I will not sign anything – No, no, keep away. I beg you, don't hit me again – "

Farrant's first blow caught him on the side of his mouth, where his beard would hide the bruises. The second landed behind his ear, another point well hidden by hair. The third was a light tap on the solar plexus, hard enough to wind, but soft enough to leave no mark.

Gasping, wiping beads of blood from his matted beard, and water from his streaming eyes, Dane stared up dazedly, helplessly, and almost unseeingly, at his tormentor.

"As long as it doesn't say I started any fires, but only that they follow me about," he muttered, "I'll sign."

   *   *   *

Thirteen miles north-east of Down Lane, in Aldgate Pump – a red-brick Victorian police station on the borders of the East End – a rather different interrogation was going on.

Matt Honiwell was chatting to Lenny Haig almost as if he were an old friend.

They were sitting, facing each other, at a plain wooden table, in an interrogation room that looked as if it had been old in Jack the Ripper's day. Four bare walls with peeling paint reared up to an immense height, to meet a cracked yellow square of ceiling. And high up on each wall there was actually an antique gas light fitting. They had been converted to electricity now, of course; bare bulbs glared unblinkingly where the gas mantles had once fizzed and spluttered. Two massive iron radiators, as antiquated as the gas fittings, only just succeeded in keeping out the dank November air.

It wasn't the cosiest of settings, but somehow its very quaintness stopped it from being wholly forbidding. That, and the fact that Honiwell had arranged for a constant supply of biscuits and coffee, and was letting Haig smoke non-stop if he pleased.

Lenny was a little man, almost of a jockey's build, who could have been almost any age between forty-five and sixty. He was actually in his middle fifties. His face – prematurely wizened, wry and monkey-like — was so unmistakably Cockney that it would have been no surprise to see him dressed up as a Pearly King. Not that there was much that was jolly about him at the moment. He was very pale and tense, and looked almost shell-shocked by what he'd been through.

"Straight up, Mr. Honiwell," he kept saying. "I'd have eat me heart out rather than get mixed up in anything like this. When I think of that poor girl half bleeding to death in hospital — "

"All right, all right, Lenny." Matt's voice was at its most gently reassuring. "I believe you. Thousands wouldn't, as they say, but I have a feeling that a jury will. I'm not really here to discuss *your* situation, but to get you to tell me as much as possible about the gang. You were sitting right in front of them up to the moment of the raid and immediately afterwards, when they were rushing back to the car in a panic for the getaway. Now I can't believe that a man with all your experience didn't get *some* clue — or can't make some pretty shrewd guesses — about the mob after going through all that with them."

Lenny stared down at a knothole on the wooden table. His manner was suddenly strained, his voice low and hoarse.

"There was five of them, o' course, I can tell you that. Two of 'em women, the rest men. Or — or boys ... The women had the revolvers, the men sawn-off shotguns."

He was clutching the edge of the table now, as though clinging on to it for dear life; and he had gone very pale.

"Bloody murdering — *gits*, the lot of them," he was muttering, almost to himself.

"Then help me to get my hands on them," Matt said gently. "Did you discover which of the five was the mob's leader?"

"Leader? Oh. Oh, yeah. I sussed that out — no bother. It was ... it was ..."

Matt was listening so intently to what Lenny was saying that he never noticed Haig's lips, and then his whole face, going a bluey grey.

The first sign he had that something was badly wrong was when the little man's head fell forward, his nose almost touching

35

the knothole.

"Lenny!" Suddenly he found himself shouting. "Lenny! What –"

He put his arms round Haig, lifted him bodily off the chair and clear of the table, and laid him out on the floor. Then he loosened his collar.

Haig's eyes flickered open.

"It's me heart, see. Always knew it was bad. Doctor used to give me pink tablets. But I've had so much on me mind . . . not been to see him for weeks . . ."

Matt Honiwell felt the world spinning round. The thought that he'd been grilling a man with a heart condition made him feel sick with shame.

All right, he'd been treating him very gently; but only hours before, he'd arrested him, pulled him in, in front of a sobbing family. The effect of this on a man already shaken up by being press-ganged into taking part in a bloodbath –

Matt took off his coat, folded it, and used it to prop up Lenny's head. Then, reaching up with one hand, he grabbed the milk jug off the table, and poured a little of the liquid down Haig's throat. It was the nearest thing to hand: it would have taken minutes to get water . . .

All the time, he talked softly, soothingly, saying anything reassuring he could think of.

"Take it easy, Lenny. Just relax. We'll have a doctor here before you can look round. And keep remembering: you're not in any real trouble. If all that you've told me is true, it'll be no time at all before all this is over and you're home again."

Haig's eyes flickered open again.

"Sorry about this, Mr. H. You're a good cop, pity there's not more like you, but this is going to look bad, isn't it? They'll say you were doing me over – doing a Rid – "

He was still trying to apologise when his eyes glazed over.

Matt rushed to the door, and shouted instructions to a constable standing outside.

"Quick. Get me some brandy, a doctor and an ambulance. In that order!"

"Yes, sir. Right away, sir ..."

The startled constable hurried away down the corridor, and returned in under five seconds with a brandy flask.

Matt took it to Haig's side.

"How are you now, Lenny?"

But Lenny was beyond hearing him.

His eyes wide with horror, he seemed to be re-living the moment when he'd heard shot after shot coming from the bank, and scream after scream of agony, all plainly audible even above the revving engine of the getaway car.

"Bloody murdering gits!" said Lenny Haig, once again.

And shaking his fist at the empty air, he died.

5 Ordeals

"I think you'll find that more congratulations are in order, sir," came the smug voice of John Farrant over the phone.

"Don't worry," said Gideon wearily. "If I do, I shall proffer them." He was beginning to be sick of Farrant's constant need of props for his self-esteem; and once again, suspicion whispered that there was something wrong with the man's mental make-up, perhaps pathologically wrong.

"I have to report that Timothy Dane has just signed a full confession," Farrant continued.

He was talking on a bad line, giving the weird impression that his enthusiasm was making the wires crackle.

"He's virtually admitted to being Dante, and to raising all fifteen of the Dante fires."

"What do you mean 'virtually'?" Gideon asked sharply. "Look. What exactly has the man admitted to?"

"He has stated (a), that he was present at all the fires, and (b), that they seem to follow him about, how or why he doesn't know. Add the facts that he is an ex-research chemist, and an ex-mental case with an obvious obsession about the very subject of 'fire' — "

"And you have pretty good grounds for getting a magistrate to commit him for trial in the morning," Gideon finished for him. "Yes. You're right, Farrant. It does seem as if you've brought off all that could be expected — and more. If you really want more congratulations from me, then you can take 'em as given."

"Thank you. Thank you very much, sir—"

"There's just one more thing."

Gideon's voice remained courteous; but there was suddenly a steely grimness behind it. Every word sliced through the crackles on the line as effortlessly as a knife through a sizzling mushroom.

"Considering the serious nature of the confession, and Dane's unbalanced mental condition, we ought to get a doctor to take a look at him as soon as possible."

"But surely, sir, we can ask the magistrate tomorrow to remand him for a medical report."

Farrant's voice held just a hint of alarm. A physical examination conducted right away might — just might — uncover traces of the battering he had given Dane, skilfully judged though the blows had been.

Gideon did not fail to notice the change in Farrant's tone. His own voice changed, too — to a roar.

"Don't you 'surely, sir' me! A mentally sick man has been subjected to heavy interrogation. He may need drugs, he may need all kinds of medical help. We owe it to ourselves — as much as to him — to make sure that he gets it, pronto. See to it right away then, will you?"

He waited until he was sure Farrant had heard, and agreed to comply. Then he slammed down the phone.

Gideon was surprised to find that he felt hot all over; that his palms were so sweaty that they had left a tiny film of moisture on the telephone receiver.

What was the matter with him? he asked himself.

He'd just heard good news, hadn't he — the best news of the day. The Dante affair — the nightmare that had given him more anxious days and nights than any other case this year — was almost over, thanks to the hard work and astuteness of John Farrant.

His congratulations shouldn't have been grudging; they should have been hearty and sincere. And he shouldn't have allowed himself to be eaten up by an illogical suspicion—

39

Suspicion. That was at the heart of the trouble, Gideon knew. Never before in his long career at the C.I.D. had he known a day when suspicion of all kinds hung so heavily in the air. There was the general, nationwide suspicion of the C.I.D. provoked by the Stannet trial, and reflected in the headlines of every newspaper. There was Scott-Marle's thinly-disguised suspicion of Riddell. There was his own suspicion of Farrant, arguably one of his most brilliant men. There was −

At that moment, the door burst open, and Matt Honiwell came in.

Gideon started to grin with relief. Sight of the homely Matt was just what he needed to remind him of the existence of that solid core of honesty, decency and humanity that remained, and always would remain the real heart of his C.I.D.

One split second later, the grin and the sense of relief were both stillborn.

Matt was paler than Gideon had ever seen him. His curly hair was wildly unkempt, falling across his forehead and even into his eyes. And he slumped into the chair opposite Gideon's desk without invitation, a thing the ordinary Matt would never have dreamed of doing.

Gideon did not admonish him. He simply went to his cubbyhole, poured Honiwell a whisky and soda, and silently pressed the glass into his hands.

"Something to do with Lenny Haig?" he asked.

Matt finished the drink at a gulp.

"Yes, George. He died on me. Right in the middle of my questioning. He had a weak heart which I didn't know about."

Matt's voice rose angrily: but the anger was directed against himself.

"Which is no excuse whatsoever, of course. I *should* have known. It should have been routine to find out about his health before I started the whole ghastly business."

Somehow he got to his feet.

"Felt I ought to come and see you personally about this, rather than say it over the phone. But I shouldn't have taken the time, really. I owe it to his wife to go and tell her what's happened without delay."

He walked across to the door, still talking.

"You know what she's going to say, don't you? She'll say that I dragged her Lenny away from her and as good as killed him. And the worst of it is, George, that *she'll be absolutely right.*"

Gideon was struggling desperately to think of something to say when one of the telephones on his desk rasped. That meant that it was the internal phone. The external ones rang.

He picked up the receiver, barked: "Can't talk now. Urgent conference," and was about to replace it on its rest when, just in time, he recognised the voice at the other end.

It was Scott-Marle.

"However urgent your conference," Sir Reginald said coldly, "I'd like you to suspend it, and come to my office straight away. I have just had the news from the Old Bailey. The jury has returned the verdict we feared: 'Not Guilty'."

Lord, thought Gideon. That was all they needed.

"I am anxious that the inquiry on Riddell should be started immediately," Scott-Marle went on, "and I have Macgregor with me now." (Macgregor was the Commander in charge of A10.) "I'd be grateful if you could help me brief him. Immediately."

No matter how urgent the summons, Gideon was not going to rush Honiwell out of his office at this crisis-point in his career.

"Give me five minutes, ten at the most," he pleaded into the phone, "and I'll be with you."

Scott-Marle did not sound pleased, but with that he had to be content.

Gideon turned to Honiwell, who was standing by the door.

"Matt, I know you. I also know how much you sympathised with Lenny Haig and his family. And believe me, being you, you simply couldn't *have helped that sympathy showing through.* In other words, it is extremely unlikely that anything you said or did seriously frightened Haig, or played any part in bringing on his heart attack."

"Then what did?" said Matt.

"Who knows? The shock and strain of the last few days . . .

41

Some conflict inside him that we don't know about ... The memory of that shoot-out ... They could all have contributed. From what you tell me, Lenny was blaming himself for being a murderer. That can be a very dangerous thing to do — and madness, when it really isn't true. Don't *you* fall into that trap, too ..."

Matt stared; then, slowly, nodded.

A little colour seeped back into his cheeks. Whether it was a delayed effect of the whisky, or the immediate effect of his homily, Gideon simply didn't know.

Matt's confidence seemed to have returned with his colour.

"The sooner I see the Haigs now, the better," he said, decisively.

Gideon made a very rare gesture. He walked with Honiwell all the way to the lift. It was the least he could do, he thought, when he was seeing a man off on the most agonising assignment of his life.

* * *

Half an hour later, when he came out of the briefing meeting with Scott-Marle and Macgregor, the A10 commander, Gideon himself faced an agonising assignment.

Tom Riddell would have returned to the Yard by now from the courtroom. He would have found a message on his desk asking him to report to Gideon. And it would be his, Gideon's, painful duty to let Tom know what he was in for.

Sure enough, when he returned to his office, he found Riddell there, waiting for him. He was prowling round the room and jumped violently when Gideon came in. Anyone who didn't know Tom's nervous temperament might well have taken even that for a guilty start.

"Sit down, man," Gideon began genially. "It's a hard life for a copper who doesn't know when to take the weight off his feet."

Riddell smiled wearily, and sank into the chair opposite Gideon's desk.

Gideon noticed that he could no more sit still than he could stand still: he kept moving his hands, shifting position, crossing and uncrossing his legs. Once again, he was uneasiness personified; *guilt* personified, his enemies would say.

"First of all, Tom, bad luck about that verdict," Gideon said. "You had a watertight case against Stannet. And it was no fault of yours that it sprang a leak."

"That's not what's worrying me," Riddell said. "The papers are implying that Stannet — and that smooth bastard Ainley — made out a watertight case against *me*. And, by implication, against the whole C.I.D. I could have scotched all that if I hadn't seized up in the witness-box. As it was, I handed the whole case to the Defence on a platter . . . God, what a mess. I suppose I ought to be grateful that no one here at the Yard suspects me. There were some moments at the Old Bailey when I actually thought I'd be suspended, and delivered to the tender mercies of A10!"

Gideon took a deep breath. This was going to be worse than he'd expected, and he'd thought he'd expected the worst.

"Well, one thing's for certain, Tom. You'll only be suspended over my dead body, and I can promise you there's a lot of life in me yet," he began heartily. "As for A10, I have to tell you that the Commissioner *has* requested them to — to make some inquiries . . ."

"*What?*"

Riddell bounded to his feet. For a moment, he looked exactly as if he was going to bring his fist crashing down on the desk-top; and Gideon remembered wryly how nearly he had assaulted Scott-Marle's desk-top, under the very same provocation, earlier that day.

He raised an eyebrow laconically.

"Hit it as hard as you want to, Tom. Might make us both feel better. I need hardly tell you that I'm as angry about it as you are. But there it is. There are two consolations. At my insistence, the inquiry will be totally confidential and very discreetly conducted. Two A10 men will be calling on you at home, after hours, to start it — tonight."

"Tonight!" Riddell gasped. "But I was going to work late here. Got a lot to catch up on after all those hours in court."

"It looks as though I'll have to order you to knock off early, then, doesn't it?"

"And let the work go hang?"

Riddell sounded bitter and weary.

"I suppose it might as well. After all, everything I've done for the past year has just gone up the spout. Sidney Stannet is sitting prettier than he was when I began investigating him. Very much prettier! He's started my own colleagues investigating *me*."

"Don't worry about Stannet," said Gideon grimly. "The day will come when we'll get him, I promise you."

Riddell smiled sourly.

"Well, let's hope that the day after that, Sir Richard bloody Ainley doesn't turn up and get him off again."

To that, Gideon had no reply.

"Who are these A10 men they've put on me?" Riddell demanded. "Am I allowed to know?"

"Of course. It's Stephenson from Uniform and Rance representing the C.I.D."

"Jimmy Rance? He was my Detective Sergeant long years ago. It was I who taught him *how* to question suspects, in the first place. I'd be interested to see how many of the tips he remembers tonight. What time are they coming, George? Have you any idea?"

"Not the faintest — but my guess would be latish: say half past nine or ten. After all, it's past seven now, and they've only just been briefed. It obviously won't be a long session: little more than a preliminary chat. It's just so that A10 can report back to Scott-Marle that they've started the inquiry without delay."

"H'm," said Riddell. "An informal preliminary chat, eh? I must say, I can't wait." He was suddenly a surprising new Riddell: cool, blandly ironical. "Should Vi and I give them sherry, or just a pot of tea?"

Vi was Riddell's little, bird-like wife — a woman whose sole interest in life was to look after her husband, and help his career. Gideon wondered suddenly how she had reacted to seeing Tom totally unjustly pilloried in the papers every day . . .

Aloud, he answered, laughing: "Either, I'm sure, would be

gratefully received.''

Even to his own ears, the laughter had a hollow ring.

He couldn't escape the feeling that Riddell was suddenly taking things too well. All those nerves, all that tension, all that bitterness couldn't have just evaporated. It must have simply sunk deeper inside him, perhaps to fester; perhaps to acquire a dangerously explosive force; perhaps to –

"I'd better be on my way," Riddell was saying.

Still unnaturally relaxed and assured, he strolled towards the door.

"Thanks for the sympathy – and good night."

"Give my regards to Vi and good – er – luck," Gideon said.

It would have been just a little tasteless to have wished Tom a good night.

*   *   *

Ten minutes later, Gideon was in his comfortable but ageing Rover, belatedly heading homewards. He should be just in time to pick up Kate and be at the Hobbses' in time for the party, which was scheduled to begin at eight.

He had the radio tuned in to a London news station, which was giving the seven-thirty headlines.

They almost all seemed to concern the C.I.D.

The first item was the "Not Guilty" verdict at the Stannet trial.

Then, rather conspicuously linked with it, came the news of the death of a man at a London police station while "helping the police with their inquiries".

It was a bare announcement. Haig's name, and the details of the case, had been withheld, of course, until the relatives had been informed. Gideon wondered grimly if this had happened; if Matt's ordeal was over yet.

Next it was announced that a man – again unnamed – had been arrested and would be charged in the morning in connection with the Dante fires. This should have cheered Gideon, but his suspicions of Farrant still made him feel uneasy rather than triumphant.

45

Finally, the "news had just come in" that Sir Reginald Scott-Marle had ordered an inquiry into the Stannet charges against – there was almost a sneer in the newscaster's voice – a "respected officer of the C.I.D."

"God knows if any of us will be respected much longer, if this sort of thing goes on," thought Gideon.

A cold gust of fury whipped through his mind, exactly matching the November gale which lashed against his windscreen, and whined round the roof of his car.

But, nearing Fulham, his whole mood changed. He thought of Alec and Penny and their happiness together – and Kate, who would by now be beside herself with excitement at the prospect of at last getting a glimpse of their daughter's new home.

These thoughts filled Gideon with a glow that momentarily melted everything else out of his mind. The house-warming was starting early, with a *Gideon*-warming, he told himself, grinning, and concentrated all his attention on hurrying home.

6 Threat

At that moment, the very last thing that Matt Honiwell was feeling was any kind of a glow.

Close on an hour had passed since he had fumblingly broken the news about Lenny Haig to his wife, Rita; but less than ten minutes had passed since she had stopped shaking, sobbing, screaming. To deepen Matt's horror, the six children had gathered round as soon as they had heard their mother crying. The Haigs' flat, above the garage business, was in the contemporary "open plan" style, with just one living space combining lounge, dining room and even kitchen. Short of banishing the kids to their bedrooms, which Matt had neither the desire nor the authority to do, there had been no way of sheltering them from the news.

Soon they all knew it; had heard their mother shriek it, sob it, over and over again.

Their father was dead.

And this bloody copper had as good as done him in.

At one point, Matt had expected all the children to launch a mass attack on him; and now he almost wished they had.

This circle of white, stunned, reproachful young faces surrounding him was more than he could bear. He knew that it would be with him in his dreams for as long as he lived.

Matt liked children: it was one of his great regrets that he had never had any of his own. He had nearly always found it easy to make them like him.

But in this situation, he felt it would be unnatural to try.

It wouldn't be right if they *didn't* hate him, after what had happened to their father.

The best thing – the only thing – was to get out of here as soon as possible.

As soon, that is, that he'd made sure of one thing.

That Rita Haig was all right now; that somehow she and all the kids would get through.

For the tenth – or it may have been the twentieth – time, he said: "Please, all of you, let me know if you feel there's anything I can do."

The circle of faces became no whit less hostile.

"You done enough, 'aintcha, copper?" Stephen, one of the elder boys, said.

"Yes," said one of his sisters, a girl of about fourteen. "Even if we was all starvin' in the gutter, we wouldn't want no bleeding help from you."

"That's enough, Liz," Rita Haig said quietly. She was a tall, striking-looking woman in her late thirties or very early forties, with dark hair and flashing eyes that suggested Spanish blood. Her earlier hysteria suggested that too; and there was also something Spanish in her present proud composure. "Whatever happened to your Dad, Mr. Honiwell here was only carrying out his job."

"'Ow do we know that?" one of the older boys demanded. "You gets to 'ear a lot of funny things about the C.I.D."

A single flash from his mother's large dark eyes silenced him.

"I think we can take his word for it," she said, still very calmly and quietly. "Look how long he's stayed here, putting up with being sworn and spat at. A bent copper would have high-tailed it down the road in thirty seconds flat."

Now the eyes were flashing Matt's way. There was actually warmth in them.

"Please stay and have a bite of supper with us, Mr. Honiwell." It was more of a command than an invitation, and she took it for granted that he would comply. She similarly ignored the resentful murmurs amongst her children, over-riding them

48

with a brisk: "Stephen, go and see what we've got in the fridge. And if there's nothing there, try the freezer. Liz, put the kettle on for tea."

*   *   *

Six fish fingers were found in the fridge. A dozen hamburgers, a six-pound packet of peas, and an avalanche of chips emerged from the freezer. Tea was made by feeding two vast brown china pots with half-a-dozen teabags each. Nobody felt like eating; but everybody was glad of something to do, and behind it all was the Cockney tradition of putting on a good show in front of a guest – even a far-from-honoured one.

No tablecloth was produced – in fact, no table was laid at all. The Haigs ate sitting on divans or armchairs around the room, each with a loaded tray balanced on his (or her) knees.

Matt was given what he imagined was the best place – the armchair nearest the T.V. – with a tray on his lap containing a plate piled with hamburgers, peas and chips; two large bottles, one of HP sauce and one of Heinz Tomato Ketchup; and what could only be described as a man-size cup of tea.

"No sense laying up for meals here," Rita said briskly. "We run a twenty-four-hour garridge business, don't we. There's always cars queuing up out there, sometimes by the dozen; and that means whatever you're eatin' has to go in and out of the oven like a bleedin' yoyo."

"Is the garage open now?"

"Nah. I sent Steve and Barb 'ere down to close it, didn't I, soon as I'd 'eard – about Lenny. We can't stay closed for more'n a night, though. Not with the bloody bills we've got to pay."

"But if they're non-stop queues of cars, night and day –"

"We must be quids in? Ah, yes, we *would* be, Mr. H, if it weren't for the fact that Lenny was a great wheeler-dealer – and never got the better of any deal! 'E ended up owing packets to 'alf the 'eavy mobs in London. And if those boys don't collect when it's due, a lorry will suddenly smash up everything in the forecourt in the middle of the night; all the tyres in our stocks

49

will mysteriously get ripped up – and that's only for starters. Yesterday, Lenny was so terrified at the thought of what one mob was trying to do that – "

"He was talked into driving that getaway car?" Matt asked softly.

There was a long pause. Gasps came from several of the children. The smallest girl – the twelve-year-old – nearly upset her tray, and stared down, aghast, at peas and fish fingers floating in an inch of tea.

"Take that out to the sink, Barb. Help yourself to fresh stuff, there's plenty more in the pans on the stove," said Rita, mechanically. Then she turned back to Matt.

"You don't miss much, Mr. H. Lenny *agreed* to drive for that mob yesterday. We cooked up that story about being held hostage by gunmen to try and cover him. Made it up on the spur of the moment, while you was 'ere."

Matt raised an eyebrow.

"Congratulations, then, on an incredibly convincing job."

"It wasn't hard to be convincing. When you think about it, more than half of what we said was true. Lenny wasn't getting a penny out of that Blackfriars snatch. He was taking part simply because he was scared not to. Scared of what that mob would do to all of us if he refused! So, really and truly, we *were* being used as hostages in a way, even though no one was actually pointing a gun at our heads. Do you see what I mean?"

"I see exactly what you mean," Matt said. "I see a lot of other things too. If Lenny did a direct deal with the Blackfriars gang, he must have known exactly who they were."

"That's right. He could have put the finger on the lot of them down there at the cop shop this arternoon. And I reckon half of him must have wanted to, to stop these 'bloody murdering gits', as he called them, once and for all."

"And you're saying the other half of him didn't want to give them away? Why not?"

Rita banged her tray down on the settee beside her. All the food on it was totally untouched; she hadn't even sipped her cup of tea. She stood up, her eyes contemptuous.

"Because Lenny's never been a squealer, that's why not. And, anyway, with the sums he owed to so many heavy mobs, it'd be nothing short of bloody suicide for him ever to turn copper's nark. *That* was what done for 'im this arternoon, Mr. H. The battle inside him over whether or not to speak was just too much for his heart, which has never been much good anyway. I realised that the moment you told me that the last thing he said was 'Bloody murdering gits . . .' "

Matt stared down at the tray on his own lap. He, too, had not touched more than a mouthful of food; but he had finished the man-sized cup of tea.

"Mrs. Haig," he said softly. "The last thing I'm here for tonight is to start any more questioning. But for all your sakes, there's one thing you must tell me. Do you, or any of your children, know any member of the Blackfriars mob by name or sight? Because if you do – and they had any reason to suppose you might put the finger on them – then you're all in very serious danger, and I must arrange immediate protection."

To his astonishment, Rita laughed – a rather cold, bitter laugh.

"If you did that, copper, they'd be sure we'd squealed. And once it got along the grapevine to the other mobs that the Haigs had started singing, we could none of us sleep safe in our beds for the rest of our lives! And the Gawd's truth of it is that Lenny kept us in the dark about everything he was mixed up with. The only villain any of us has ever sighted is a man who comes round the garridge, regular as clockwork on the first Thursday of every month, asking for five 'undred nicker. And whoever's behind the till gives it to him straight out of Wednesday's takings. There's always just about enough."

Matt started. Something had just occurred to him.

"Tomorrow's the first Thursday of the month. Sure there'll be enough in the till in the morning? Don't forget you've closed early today."

For a moment, a flicker of fear showed in Rita's eyes. Matt felt suddenly not only sympathy, but a deep admiration. This woman had lived for years, brought up her whole unruly brood, always on the edge of a precipice of terror. And even on this night of tragedy there was no let-up for her. She had to keep walking warily, making sure she toed every possible line.

In point of fact, there was probably no danger to the Haigs even if they didn't pay up in the morning. Even heavy mobs had a heart. But it wasn't a risk Matt liked the thought of her taking.

"What time does this collector come? After the banks open?"

"Yeah. Around eleven thirty to twelve. So that's the answer, copper. One of us can go and draw the money out of our account."

Matt tensed.

"Is it a joint account – in both yours and Lenny's name?"

"Nah. He'd never let me put my nose in his business. Why? What's that to you?"

"Nothing," said Matt. "Except that if it isn't a joint account, it'll be frozen now Lenny's dead. You won't be able to draw a thing."

Rita's eyes widened in something not far from terror.

"Cripes. That's bloody torn it, ain't it? We're all for the f-----g high jump, then."

Matt put his tray of hamburgers gently on the ground, and stood up, his own cheque-book in his hand.

"*My* account isn't frozen," he said softly. "And luckily, my branch is in easy reach. Will three hundred see you through?"

He was well aware that he was breaking all the rules. But it was a very short-term loan; the Haigs could probably pay it back out of their takings in twenty-four hours. And the overwhelming relief which showed in Rita's eyes was a very adequate reward.

When Matt left the Haigs, ten minutes later, the whole family was gathering round him, treating him almost like a close and trusted friend. Which did not stop him from having a queasy feeling of guilt and shame as he went out to his car.

The November gale was getting stronger every minute, and hit him with biting force as he crossed the garage forecourt. Around him tin signs advertising motor oils and special offers clattered and clanked in a mournful chorus; and up on the roof of the garage building, above the Haigs' flat, a monstrous metal globe selling GLOBALPOWER, a new American petrol, joined in with an ominous creaking.

The cruel basic fact hadn't changed, they seemed to be reminding him, with cold, metallic emphasis. Lenny Haig was still dead. And he was still the copper who had as good as done him in.

*　　*　　*

About an hour later, in the warmth of his cosy little Bayswater flat, Matt's dark self-accusations at last began to fade. He had poured them all out to Netta, the woman he lived with and thought of as his wife; and Netta had a wonderful way of making him feel at peace with himself and the world again, usually with a very few words.

"With a heart like that, and under all these pressures, Lenny was lucky to have lasted as long as he did," she said firmly. "He might have gone any time, Matt. You were just unlucky enough to be there when it happened. And who else at the Yard would have done as much as you did to make amends? I'm only afraid that — "

She broke off sharply.

"That what?" Matt said.

"That — " Netta's high forehead creased into a faint frown " — you might have gone *too* far."

Matt laughed.

"In lending them three hundred quid? Love, that's nothing these days. Half a day's takings at the Haig garage. We'll be paid back before — "

It was at that moment that the telephone rang.

Still chatting, Matt walked across the lounge to answer it.

" — before tomorrow night, or Friday at the latest. I know I was bending the rules a bit, but there simply wasn't anything else I could ... Hullo. Honiwell here."

"Good evening, Mr. Honiwell."

It was a thick, jeering voice, and muffled, almost as though the speaker had put a handkerchief over the mouthpiece.

"I'll come straight to the point. Rita Haig tells me that you've

53

just been to see her. In the presence of her whole family – who will all testify to the fact – you admitted leaning a bit heavily on Lenny Haig. And then you gave them £300 to keep their mouths shut." The voice became rougher, openly insolent and jeering. "Well, it's not enough, copper. You'll have to do a lot more than that to keep your nose clean and your name out of the papers. For instance, I suggest that you and the whole f------ police force should lay off the Haigs, and give them and their garage a very wide berth from now on. And if I were you, I'd think very hard before I asked any more nasty, nosey questions about what happened yesterday in the Blackfriars Road ... Just a word to the wise, copper. That's all."

A final, thick chuckle was cut short as the line went dead.

7 The Police's Police

For several seconds, Matt stood motionless by the phone. Sweat broke out all over him, but his brain seemed to be giving one set of orders to his glands and another to his internal thermostat. He felt not feverishly hot, but depthlessly, glacially cold.

"As Rita Haig would put it," he said very, very softly, " 'That's torn it, ain't it?' "

He repeated the gist of the call to Netta, adding: "It's not difficult to see what's happened. The Blackfriars mob has just paid a visit to the Haigs. Probably they've been watching the garage, and knew the moment I'd left. They'd be desperately anxious to find out about Lenny, and if he'd done any squealing. Rita Haig obviously told them everything I'd said and done and they realised immediately that they'd got me where they wanted me."

"But you never 'leaned heavily' on Lenny. You couldn't possibly have admitted doing anything of the sort."

"What I said . . . and what the Blackfriars mob *can scare the Haigs into swearing that I said* . . . are two very different things, love. And almost anybody would take that cheque as proof positive that something shady was going on."

Matt's normally quiet, relaxed voice suddenly rose a couple of octaves, and became almost a hysterical shout.

"Stannet and his bent barrister crony have made mincemeat of Tom Riddell without having a single scrap of evidence against him. With that cheque in their hands and the Haigs under their thumb, there are absolutely no limits to what the Blackfriars gang can do to *me*!''

Netta – a tall, attractive woman, not unlike Gideon's Kate – remained calm and cool. Whatever the crisis, she nearly always did. Perhaps this was because of her background. Long years of trying to cope with a dipsomaniac husband, and all those subsequent years of living with Matt but being unable to marry him because that husband had refused a divorce – all this had taught Netta a lot about how to be patient, how to endure and how never to give in.

"If I were you," she murmured, "I'd hear what George has to say about all this before you get too despairing."

Matt flung himself wearily into an armchair.

"If the Blackfriars mob gets the Haigs to tell this story to the papers, there's nothing even George can do to help me. The case would go straight to Scott-Marle, and from him to A10."

"What's A10? You've mentioned them before, but I've never really understood."

Matt leaned back in the armchair, and closed his eyes. He looked what he was: emotionally and nervously exhausted, and very close to admitting total defeat.

"A10 are the police's police. Coppers compelled to spend two years spying on fellow coppers. I've heard some odd stories about them. They all start out hating the job, but after a few months, some of them get hooked on it. I've a few friends who've been honoured with their attentions. They say the Spanish Inquisition isn't in it."

An idea struck him, and he opened his eyes. There was a bleakness in them now; the bleakness of despair.

"Of course, at my age, I can resign whenever I want to. Perhaps that wouldn't be a bad idea, love. Then someone new can take over the case, someone who hasn't blotted his copybook. And I shan't give a toss whatever A10 – or the papers – say."

Netta's heart leaped. She had secretly wanted Matt to resign for a long time.

There were new divorce laws now: in less than three months they would at last be free to marry, and they'd planned a very,

very quiet wedding at the Kensington Registry Office. It would be wonderful if they could make that day the start of a new life, free from the worries and tensions inescapable from C.I.D. work in these days of sophisticated criminals and easily-twisted laws.

But as soon as the thought entered her head, Netta knew that she must reject it. If she allowed him to quit – to retire under a cloud, almost in disgrace – then she would have to live for the rest of her life with a defeated Matt Honiwell.

A defeated Matt Honiwell?

The very phrase was an absurdity, a contradiction in terms.

This despair that had taken him over was purely momentary, the result of the endless succession of shocks he had sustained on this traumatic day.

At least, Netta told herself, it *would* be momentary if she could only think of something to shake him out of the mood, before it took any sort of a hold on his mind.

Suddenly, instinctively, she knew the right thing to say.

Deliberately using the last words of Lenny Haig, as Matt had described them to her a few minutes before, she said – her normally gentle voice now harsh and challenging: "So you're really going to let yourself be beaten by a lot of – *bloody murdering gits?*"

From the way Matt came bounding out of his chair, she knew that she had her answer.

*   *   *

At that precise moment, in their comfortable semi-detached in Wembley, Tom and Vi Riddell were also talking about A10.

It would have been odd if they had been discussing anything else, because at any moment, Riddell was expecting two A10 men – Stephenson from Uniform and Rance from the C.I.D. – to knock at the door.

Yet, curiously enough, he felt no alarm at the prospect at all. His nerves, which had tortured him and left him tongue-tied and nearly fainting in the witness-box that very morning, now seemed so completely numb that he might have been anaesthetised.

He was delighted and astonished at his own calmness; at the casual ease with which he was setting out to soothe Vi's fears.

"There's nothing to worry about *whatsoever*, dear. Everybody at the C.I.D. knows perfectly well that the Stannet-Ainley accusations against me are frame-ups. And all these A10 men are going to do is help me prove it! Don't you see, they're friends, not enemies . . . and Jimmy Rance, of course, is a very old friend indeed. As I was telling George Gideon this evening, I taught Jimmy everything he knows about interrogation."

Vi fixed him with an anxious, angry eye, exactly like that of a mother bird surprised in its nest.

"So they're going to interrogate you? Here, tonight? After all those hours you've had in the witness-box these last few days? I never heard of anything so outrageous – "

Riddell burst out laughing, though he was by no means sure what at.

"According to George, this visit might well be just a preliminary chat."

Vi was not consoled.

"You mean, this is only the beginning? It's all going on for night after night after night?" She was staring up at him beseechingly, and almost crying. "Tom, you know what state your nerves are in. You're simply not going to be able to stand it."

Once again, Riddell surprised himself by laughing.

"Look, love. I did all the cracking up I'm going to do in the Old Bailey this morning. I feel fine now, I promise you. Absolutely fine, and ready to take on anything."

Why was she looking at him so worriedly? Couldn't she tell that he was speaking the plain and simple truth?

He was still trying to puzzle it out when Vi interrupted his thoughts with an urgent whisper.

"Sh. Listen . . ."

Through a sudden lull in the blustery winds buffeting the house, her sharp ears had picked up the sound of a car pulling up outside.

It looked as though the police's police had arrived.

Five minutes passed, though, before there was a knock on the Riddell's door, because there was a heated altercation going on in the A10 car.

Throughout the journey, Chief Superintendent Robert Stephenson had been giving vent to his suspicions of Riddell, while Chief Detective Superintendent James Rance had been maintaining that Tom really had no case to answer.

The argument had come to a head just as Stephenson, who was driving, had drawn into the kerb and pulled up. (On informal night visits, A10 men didn't use drivers.)

"It's just not good enough, Jimmy boy, to assume that a case is flimsy just because you happen to have known and liked Riddell," he stated flatly. "Oh, I can't blame you C.I.D. people for sticking together. But just remember, lad," he finished ponderously, indicating the sleeve of his smart blue uniform, "this material is proof against that sort of glue!"

Jimmy Rance groaned. He liked and respected Stephenson, but there was no denying that, like so many Uniform men, he had a massive chip on his shoulder about the C.I.D.

Probably it wasn't surprising. Stephenson, a long, lean, leathery-faced man in his middle-to-late fifties, had been pounding a beat in the 1940s, and had earned all his promotions the hard way, each forward step taking many painful years. Rance, plump, fresh-complexioned and at least twenty years Stephenson's junior, had not joined the police until the late 1960s and, getting into the C.I.D., had risen from Detective Sergeant to Chief Detective Superintendent in less than a decade. In Stephenson's eyes, he was, therefore, the living proof of how unfairly the promotion scales were weighted the C.I.D. man's way. In the past, this had not led to great tension between them; Stephenson had taken the old soldier's line: "You've had it easy, but good luck to you, mate." But this case was different, because Rance had rashly admitted how much of his quick promotion he had owed to Tom Riddell's help and encouragement. Stephenson had immediately suspected a C.I.D. plot to undermine the whole A10 inquiry. Suspicion heightened by jealousy, jealousy intensified by suspicion – all this was mounting inside

59

him, making him a sour companion indeed.

In point of fact, Macgregor, the astute – and, incidentally, uniformed – A10 commander, had chosen Jimmy Rance for this assignment precisely because of his friendly relationship with Riddell.

When a policeman's character and integrity is being attacked on a nation-wide scale, it is only evening things up a little to give him a firm friend at court. That was the way Macgregor had seen it. And the selection of Bob Stephenson had been no accident either. As the most violently anti-C.I.D. man attached to A10, his presence guaranteed that things weren't evened up too much.

In other words, the A10 commander had deliberately chosen an explosively-mixed investigating team: and the explosion did not look as if it would be long delayed.

Bob Stephenson leant back in the driving-seat, switched off the engine, and folded his arms.

"Before either of us take a step out of this car, Rance, I want your assurance that you'll be taking a totally impartial attitude from now on. One more of your prejudicial 'Poor old Tom' remarks, and I'll – "

The wind roaring over the roof of the car made the rest of the sentence inaudible. Just as well, thought Jimmy Rance grimly. It had sounded like a threat, and under no circumstances would he work with a colleague who threatened. As it was, he never remembered a case where he had to keep such a tight rein on his temper.

"So I'm prejudiced, am I?" he barked, his tone biting enough to carry effortlessly through the sounds of the gale. "Then just run your clear-sighted, dispassionate eyes over this, old chummy." He whipped a tattered typewritten sheet from his breast pocket and held it virtually under Stephenson's nose. "It's a list of Stannet and Ainley's star witnesses. 'Nosey' Knowles, who testified that Tom had slipped him £1000 to shop Stannet. Slim O'Casey, who swore that Tom had blackmailed him into forging Stannet's name on an incriminating letter. Ned Morris, who claimed that Tom had blacked his eyes and beaten him up during a questioning ... Do you claim it's pure coincidence that all three are known to have been on the Stannet payroll for years?'' Another gust of wind whipped round the car. But Jimmy was determined not to be silenced, not even by Nature at its stormiest. His bark became a yell that sounded loud enough to shatter the windscreen. ''And it's on this slippery trio – and a few more like them – that *Stannet's whole case rests*! Do you deny that? If so, it's not me who's being blind and deaf and dumb with prejudice – it's YOU!''

He broke off, breathless. There wasn't much point in going on. Stephenson had simply clapped his hands over his ears.

''I'm not listening to any facts that don't emerge in the course of our inquiry,'' he said, stolidly. ''And that inquiry doesn't begin until we're over there, knocking on the subject's door. Shall we go?''

''Not just yet,'' Rance said breathlessly. He was having a battle now to prevent himself from seizing the old devil and shaking him until he rattled from the toes of his regulation boots to the peak of his regulation cap. ''I'd like to remind you that our 'subject', as you call him, has had a long, rough day and is probably nearly a nervous wreck. Let's keep this first session very short, shall we – and, if you can possibly manage it, not too sharp.''

He expected an abrasive, perhaps even an abusive retort. He forgot that no one who has spent long years pounding a beat ever wholly ceases to be human.

Bob Stephenson's leathery face cracked into a grin.

''Motion carried unanimously, young fellow. It's late. It's a stinking night. And I'm not for kicking a man when he's down any more than you are. The only reason I'll stay longer than five minutes is if Mrs. Riddell comes up with a smashing cup of char.''

A moment later, the tension between them temporarily slackened, the two A10 men were battling their way up the trim gravel path to the Riddells' door. One of the worst gusts of the night hit them when they were about halfway. On their right, a rose bush swayed unnaturally across the path, clawing at their clothing like a wildcat. Somewhere to their left, behind a garage, came the deafening crash of a dustbin overturning, followed by a long-continuing clatter as its lid rolled round and round the Riddells' backyard.

The front door was open before they reached it. They rushed inside, breathless and panting, and the door was closed behind them. They looked round, blinking, and saw the gaunt but still massive frame of Tom Riddell. Vi — bird-like as ever — appeared and darted to his side.

"Good evening, gentlemen," Riddell said genially. "Nice to see you again, Jimmy. And — " he turned to the tall uniformed figure " — you're Bob Stephenson, aren't you? I've heard a great deal about you over the years. But I don't believe we've ever met before."

"No, sir." Stephenson was back to being coldly, aggressively formal. "I don't believe we have."

Riddell ignored the formal tone.

"Well, go inside and make yourselves at home. Vi here has put a kettle on."

Smiling smoothly, he gestured towards the doorway of the lounge. He looked, to Rance, almost too relaxed and assured. His face had a high colour; there was a glint in his eyes that was not far from feverish. All very unlike the usual Tom Riddell . . .

Rance shrugged. He wasn't here as a doctor, but as an inquisitor. A pointless, impertinent inquisitor. Uneasy and embarrassed, he made to follow Stephenson into the lounge, an attractive room with an old-fashioned fireplace, carefully preserved, and a real log fire burning in the grate.

Just as Rance reached the lounge doorway, the November wind renewed its fury. The fire sputtered and spread smoke all over the room. A dull, floor-shaking thud suggested that something big had fallen down outside: perhaps a clothes-line post, perhaps a fence, perhaps even a tree.

"Christ!" said Riddell, behind them. "If you'll excuse me for a moment, I'd better just make sure the sky hasn't fallen in on us."

He opened the front door and slipped out, closing it behind

him.

Rance walked on into the lounge, where Stephenson was enthusiastically poking the fire.

"Takes me back a bit, this does," he said, contentedly. "Not seen a fire like this since – oh, it must be the early sixties."

Vi came in carrying a tray, with a silver teapot, cups, saucers, a jug of milk and a plate of assorted biscuits.

Stephenson's eyes lit up at the sight of the tea.

"Very kind of you, Mrs. Riddell. Very kind of you in – "

He broke off as the wind outside rose again, and this time seemed to be making the most curious sound yet: a creaking, followed by a metallic click, as though a big door had been swung open and fixed into place.

Rance, who was looking closely at Vi's face at that moment, saw her eyes widen in bewilderment and disbelief.

He wasn't sure – it had been hard to make out anything much in that wild stormy darkness – but he rather believed that the Riddells' garage had an "up and over" door, which would have swung open with just that sound.

The next seconds confirmed all his suspicions. There came the unmistakable sound of a car starting up immediately outside.

"*Tom!*"

It was a despairing wail from Vi. The tray dropped from her hands. Stephenson caught it before it reached the carpet, but was too late to stop the pot falling on its side, and tea spilling all over the tray.

"Tom!" Vi wailed again, her voice almost drowned by the roar of the car as it went charging down the drive and out into the street at all of fifty miles an hour. A grating clatter joined the odd noises of this surrealistic night, and Rance realised that their own car must have been partly blocking the exit from the drive. Riddell was in such a blind panic to get away that he had taken their rear light and half a mudguard with him, from the sound of it.

"You must stop him!" Vi was almost screaming. "He – he might kill somebody!"

"Very possibly," Stephenson answered levelly. "But we're

not here to apprehend your husband, Mrs. Riddell, merely to ask him a few informal questions. It's his privilege not to answer them, and even to refuse to see us."

"But, he's not himself!" Vi shouted. "I don't think – I honestly don't think he knows what he's doing."

Almost in slow motion, Stephenson put the tray down on to a coffee-table.

"Let's hope he doesn't, Mrs. Riddell," he said gravely.

Then, with a lifetime's hatred of the C.I.D. putting a wealth of hidden relish behind every syllable, he added: "Because what he's doing is losing all possible chance of remaining Chief Detective Superintendent Riddell, as even his old friend, Mr. Rance here, must agree."

Jimmy Rance's plump features reddened, but he kept silent for the simplest and most shattering of reasons.

Suddenly there was nothing in the world that he could say.

8 House-warming

Gideon had not enjoyed himself so much for years.

He had half-expected Alec and Penny's house-warming party to be a rather formal occasion, perhaps with a number of Alec's relatives whom he hardly knew, or – even worse – a lot of Penny's highbrow musical friends.

To his astonishment (and secret relief) he found that it wasn't that sort of affair at all. Alec, with his strenuous work at the Yard and Penny, with her big programme of concert engagements just ahead, had not been in the mood for large-scale socialising. All they had really wanted to do was reward Kate and Gideon for containing their curiosity about the house, and resisting the temptation to pry or spy. And the best reward they could think of was to give them a full-scale private view, with all the trimmings.

The "party", in fact, was simply a quiet family dinner, with Gideon and Kate as the only guests; and never in their lives had they felt such honoured ones.

The house – a detached Edwardian villa, built almost in Colonial style, with a wide verandah and white weatherboarding covering the upper storeys – was impressive enough on the outside. But inside it was positively breathtaking. Every room looked as if it had come straight out of *Homes and Gardens*; every piece of furniture – from the baby grand piano in the living room to a splendid eighteenth-century warming pan hanging in the hall – reflected both Alec's sense of elegance and Penny's unfailingly good taste. "Reflected" was the right word: everything had been polished until one could literally see one's face in it.

And Kate's face was worth seeing a dozen times over tonight, Gideon thought. Her blue-grey eyes, usually so calm, were shining with an almost schoolgirlish excitement; and there was also something schoolgirlish about the way she rushed from room to room, one minute praising the choice of curtain material, the next testing the softness of a Continental quilt, and the next being lost in admiration of a quartz carriage clock. But no schoolgirl could have equalled the languid grace with which Kate's tall, slim body moved; and for that matter, thought Gideon, no other woman he had ever met could equal it either. It was unique to Kate, that *flowing* way of moving, and never altered, no matter how many years went by.

After a happy hour of viewing and admiring came a sumptuous dinner served in a dining room lit only by candles. In a magic atmosphere of soft light, and shadows dancing over gleaming mahogany, Gideon and Kate had been treated to home-made leek soup, a delicious *Boeuf Strogonoff* and a light-as-a-feather lemon sorbet, followed by coffee and fine old cognac. Then they went into the living room to hear Penny play "a little something" on the baby grand. This turned out to be Chopin's "Polonaise"; and although played now with flawless professionalism, it sent nostalgic memories flooding through Gideon's brain. It had been one of Penny's party pieces when she was quite small, and it took him back to the days when she had played it far from flawlessly, banging it out on the battered old family piano, in blithe defiance of the racket made by her two sisters and three brothers as they rampaged around the room. Gideon couldn't deny that he would give a great deal to be able to turn the clock back to those days, when his home – a solid, red-brick Victorian house in Harringdon Road, Fulham – teemed with bustling family life. Those may have been hectic, harassing, occasionally even harrowing times, but at least the basic issues had been simple and clear-cut. He had had to try to be a good father to his family; he had had to try to be a kind of father to the C.I.D., guiding it, governing it, guarding it as it spearheaded London's fight against crime.

Now everything was different and very little was simple and clear-cut at all. The family was scattered far and wide and didn't often need his help. And the C.I.D. was in deep water, facing problems which it was beyond his power – beyond any Commander's power – to cure.

All any police force could do, when it had caught its man, was to hand him over to the law. But if the law was unable to convict even on watertight evidence; if honest C.I.D. men like Riddell found themselves maligned and subjected to A10 inquiries the moment they got back to the Yard, then there was no way to stop cynicism and defeatism spreading like a canker throughout the C.I.D. And with that defeatism, as surely as night followed day, would come more and more corruption.

Gideon didn't like the prospect, and relished least of all the dismaying sense of helplessness with which it filled him. Everywhere he looked, it seemed, there was nothing he could do.

There was nothing he could do, for example, about the Riddell business. He had stopped Tom being suspended; he had even given him a surreptitious hand by asking Macgregor of A10 to consider putting Jimmy Rance on the case. But he couldn't stop the A10 inquiry, no matter what it did to Tom's self-confidence: and of course, he couldn't stop Stannet, one of the most vicious villains on the London scene, walking away completely free.

Then there was the Blackfriars snatch case. He hadn't mentioned the fact to Matt Honiwell, who was already suffering from such a heavy load of remorse, but the death of Lenny Haig was an extremely awkward thing to have happened at this particular moment. The Stannet case was not yet out of the headlines; suspicion of the C.I.D. was widespread and mounting. If the Haig family started a public outcry, then many a Fleet Street editor might be tempted to jump on the band-wagon and back them. In which case, unless Matt watched his step extremely carefully, he himself might be facing suspension and/or an A10 inquiry. And Matt was altogether too human a policeman to watch his step when faced with a bereaved family.

Gideon suddenly sensed that Honiwell might be heading into serious trouble – and if he was, once again, there was nothing he could do.

As if these anxieties weren't gnawing deep enough into his peace of mind, there was the Timothy Dane business. It looked as if Farrant had arrested the right man, and the confession seemed to confirm it; but that didn't prevent Gideon feeling deeply uneasy about the whole affair. He tried hard to shrug the feeling off. The Dale arrest had been a sensational success, the one C.I.D. triumph in an otherwise disastrous day. Did he *have* to look such a splendid gift horse in the mouth?

Penny was bringing the "Polonaise" to a splendid conclusion, its final crashing chords ringing through the room with the clarity and force of a peal of cathedral bells. Kate and Alec burst into spontaneous clapping, and Gideon, reddening at the thought that he had hardly heard a note of the performance, made up for it by applauding longest and loudest of all.

Penny stood up and, laughing, acknowledged his efforts with a little curtsy in his direction. Often clumsy and even gawky in the past, Penny was now beginning to move with just a touch of her mother's grace.

"Anybody want the ten o'clock news?" she asked, and moved across to the television set, an expensive one, with the screen concealed behind carved wooden doors.

"Oh, no," Kate pleaded. "Let's take a rest from the news tonight."

Gideon was momentarily tempted to agree. For once, it was his deputy who refused to turn a deaf ear to the call of duty.

"We daren't, I'm afraid," Alec told Kate with an apologetic smile. "Just at the moment, the C.I.D. seems to *be* the news."

But when, a couple of seconds later, the set glowed into life, it looked as though he was wrong.

The newscaster was talking about a union dispute. Quite a serious dispute, apparently. Negotiations were still continuing, but had reached the "last-ditch" stage. And if they broke down, a full-scale strike was scheduled to begin in, as the newscaster put it, piling on the drama, "just twenty-six hours' time, at twelve midnight tomorrow.''

Gideon listened with only perfunctory interest. Strikes were often a headache for Uniform; occasionally, if violent political activists were concerned, they might involve Special Branch; but only on very rare occasions was the C.I.D. drawn in. The last time he remembered that happening was when a Customs strike gave certain big smuggling operators the opportunity of a lifetime.

The programme producer had cut from the newscaster to the spokesman for the strikers, who was taking the usual "this-hurts-us-more-than-it-hurts-you" Union line, but seemed to be showing more genuine regret than usual, even a touch of anguish.

"Of course we realise that lives may be lost as a result of our action," he was saying. "But when it comes to the crunch, at the end of the day . . ."

The Union jargon was so over-familiar that Gideon did not know whether to groan or to grin.

". . . the responsibility can only be laid in one place: squarely on the Government's doorstep," the man was finishing; and suddenly Gideon was on the edge of his chair, staring tensely at the set.

Up till now the man had been purely a talking head on the screen; but now the camera tracked back slightly, showing neck, shoulders, collar, tie. Gideon realised that he was in uniform – a uniform he knew almost as well as that of a London bobby.

The man was a member of – and obviously speaking on behalf of – the London Fire Brigade.

And if *they* were going on strike from midnight tomorrow, then the question of whether or not Farrant had arrested the right man took on a life-or-death importance. Because if Dante was still on the loose . . .

Gideon had a sudden vision of the army, with its untrained, unskilled firefighters and antiquated "Green Goddess" fire-engines, trying to combat even one of Dante's spectacular chemical blazes. And there was no guarantee that there would only be one. The man was clever and adroit enough to light half-

69

a-dozen, perhaps circling the city with a ring of fires which, given this raging wind, could spread like lightning until —

For all the world like an alarm clock waking him out of a nightmare, the telephone rang in the Hobbs's hall.

Alec strolled out to answer it, but he was not strolling when he came back. He almost rushed into the room, his expression as tense as Gideon's.

"It's Jimmy Rance, George. Wants to talk to you about Riddell — I gather, very urgently indeed."

*   *   *

By an odd coincidence, the T.V. news programme had switched to the Stannet case. A commentator was saying: "This case raises disturbing questions for us all."

But not half as many disturbing questions, thought Gideon grimly, as this announcement raised for him. Rance was not on his staff at the moment. He was attached to A10, and A10 men were not allowed to communicate details of their inquiries to anyone except their commander.

It was an important rule, essential to A10's functioning as an impartial inquiry unit, and Gideon did not see how he could face Macgregor — or Scott-Marle, for that matter — in the morning, if he allowed it to be broken. On the other hand, if Tom was in some new trouble . . .

He glanced at Hobbs, who immediately understood his problem, and typically, had already dealt with it.

"Don't worry, George. I told Rance he had no business to be contacting either you or me about Riddell, but he says he's already spoken to Macgregor, and was positively *ordered* to ring you. They told him at the Yard, of course, where you were."

Gideon's eyes widened. Macgregor would only have broken such a fundamental rule in the most extreme emergency.

A moment later, three strides had taken him out into the hall, and he was picking up the phone.

"Gideon here. What's happened, Jim?"

Rance, who was speaking from the Riddells' home, egged on by a glowering Bob Stephenson, sounded hoarse and excited as he spelled out the facts. *Over*-excited, Gideon thought, when he had heard what he had to say. Rance was a good detective, and was undoubtedly trying to do his best for Riddell; but he always had tended to make too much of a meal of everything. Small wonder he was so fat . . .

"Commander Macgregor told me to ring you, sir," he finished breathlessly, "because if Tom *is* in a dangerous condition – "

"Dangerous?" said Gideon. "Because he decided to go for a run in his car instead of facing a lot of tomfool questions? From what you tell me, Rance, that's really all that happened, and I can't honestly say that it sounds particularly dangerous to me."

There was a startled pause while Rance recovered from the rebuff. Gideon could imagine his plump features turning crimson at the other end of the line.

"But he was driving totally recklessly," Rance said at length.

"Or purposefully, depending on how you look at it," Gideon said. "He was obviously secretly very angry about your visit, and your car was blocking the exit from his drive. I can imagine him saying to himself, 'This serves those bastards right'."

He realised that he was close to chuckling, which, in the circumstances, really wouldn't do. More soberly, he added: "Don't get me wrong, Jim. I'm not condoning Riddell's conduct. It was reprehensible, to put it mildly. All I'm pointing is that after all he's been through today, it isn't too difficult to understand. And I can't see there's any reason to assume that he's had a brainstorm, or gone berserk, or – "

"But that's Mrs. Riddell's opinion, sir," Rance said. "She believes that he simply doesn't know what he's doing."

"Then please put her on the line," Gideon said.

This was more worrying. No wife in the world was more devoted to her husband than the little, bird-like Vi was to Tom Riddell. The last thing she'd be likely to do was tell tales about his state of mind to the Commander of the C.I.D. Unless something had really frightened her, and she was really terrified about what he might do . . .

Suddenly he remembered his talk with Riddell at Scotland Yard, less than three hours before. He thought of Tom's

71

uncanny relaxed assurance and his own queer feelings that behind it, all that bitterness and tension must be festering, and might be building into something sinister.

A new voice came on the line; and it wasn't Vi Riddell's. It was deep and so unmistakably Uniform that Gideon had no trouble identifying it as Stephenson's.

"I'm afraid Mrs. Riddell is unable to come to the phone, sir, due to her own overwrought condition. If you would like my views on Riddell's state, it is my belief that for his own sake, and for the public safety, immediate steps should be taken to – "

Gideon's exasperation boiled over.

"When I need advice on what steps to take, I'll have dancing lessons!" he roared. "Will you please try again to bring Mrs. Riddell to the phone – to speak to my wife, if not to me."

Kate knew Vi Riddell quite well. She had spent long hours comforting her, when Riddell had been rushed to hospital, after his battle to save an immigrant family in a collapsing house – the exploit that had nearly won him a George Medal. Gideon remembered that even in the course of that case – eight, nine years ago now – Vi had been worried that Tom might be heading for a nervous breakdown.

Could his mind have snapped at last? It wasn't impossible, Gideon supposed. But that still didn't make him a public menace, a cause for "immediate steps to be taken".

He could hear a woman's sobs in the background on the other end of the line, and Rance saying: "It's not the Commander, Mrs. Riddell. It's *Mrs.* Gideon who wants to talk to you."

Cue for exit, if he ever heard one, Gideon told himself. He hurried into the living room, and asked Kate to go to the phone, explaining the situation in a few terse sentences.

Kate had a marvellous touch with human problems, although, like Matt Honiwell, she could become too upset by them, too emotionally involved.

She hurried out into the hall, and within a few minutes, was working the old Kate magic, telling Vi not to worry; she was sure Tom would be his old self again in no time, now that the Stannet case and all its problems were over. She even offered to drive to

Wembley and stay with Vi for the night, but both agreed that that wasn't a good idea. Riddell might just be coasting around the neighbourhood in his car, waiting until his interrogators had left. If he came home and found Gideon's wife there, it might prove the very last straw.

When Kate put down the phone, Vi was a lot calmer; but Kate herself was looking worried, strained.

"She's totally baffled, George, and very scared. Tom's never been anything like this before. He was so calm and cheerful tonight, and yet his eyes were strange, she said. Feverish. Once or twice, he looked right through her as if she wasn't there. I don't like the sound of it at all. A man in a state like that, driving around at fifty miles an hour at the minimum, and this wild night can't be helping."

Gideon glanced at his watch.

"Tom left at about nine thirty, I gather. Well, it's now ten fifteen. He's been driving for three quarters of an hour, and if he's in as bad a way as all that, there are bound to have been incidents . . ." He glanced up at Hobbs who, all this time, had been standing silently in a corner of the hall, arms folded, just listening. "Don't you agree, Alec?"

"I certainly do," Hobbs said. "And they could have happened anywhere over a forty-mile radius. I'll check with the Yard."

He walked across to the phone, a dutiful Deputy Commander. Before picking up the receiver, he paused, and became a courteous host.

"Leave this to me, George. You and Kate go back into the living room. Penny's dying to serve up her new-style Continental coffee. It's the kind with a percolating filter on every cup."

Gideon was about to revolt, but then he remembered that he *was* a guest.

He laughed, and gave Kate his arm.

"Café Continental, it seems, dear, is just this way."

He and Kate had barely returned to their chairs in the living room when the door burst open, and Alec came striding in from the hall.

Gideon had rarely seen him looking so shaken.

"You were right, George. There has been an incident, but not a traffic one. The Yard says that Riddell called in there in person about a quarter of an hour ago."

"Did he seem – all right?" Kate asked.

Alec's voice became a tense, dry drawl.

"A little strange, the sergeant at the desk says. But he didn't stay long enough for anybody to notice much about him. He left again inside a couple of minutes – after going down to the stores. and drawing out a revolver."

9 Rough Nights

There was a long pause, broken only by the whistling of the wind. It was now blowing such a gale outside that not even the expensive double glazing which the Hobbses had installed could keep out all the sound, though it *did* subdue it, to the level of waves lashing on some faraway shore.

Alec started pacing up and down the room, his face expressionless, double-glazed, as it were, against the storms inside him. "There's not much doubt what we've got to do," he said. "And we're not going to enjoy doing any of it. Tom has obviously blown his top, and is hell-bent on taking the law into his own hands. That means, as I see it, that we've got (a) to suspend him immediately as Detective Chief Superintendent; (b) to start an immediate search for him, using as many men or women as we can spare, and (c) to provide police protection for Stannet, Sir Richard Ainley and all the key witnesses who spoke against Riddell at the trial. It goes deeply against the grain, using the law to protect these lousy law-twisters, but do we have a choice?"

Gideon leant back in his armchair which, although part of a brand-new suite, creaked slightly beneath his weight. He put his hand in his pocket, until his fingers found and cradled the bowl of an old briar pipe. He never smoked it now, but for some reason always fingered it at moments of crisis. He was well aware that he was about to take one of the riskiest decisions of his career.

"Yes," he said quietly. "I think we *do* have a choice, Alec.

75

And for once – for the first time in years, I believe – my choice is not yours."

He stood up and walked to the windows. Behind the curtains, he could hear leaves and twigs scratching furiously against the pane. The gale was turning the whole world crazy and wild out there tonight.

Gideon swung round to face the room. Alec, Kate, Penny – all of them were peering at him intently, almost breathlessly.

"I've been saying this all day in one way or another, but no one seems to understand," Gideon said. "The Stannet trial has made the whole nation suspicious of Riddell, and in spite of ourselves, we could be letting those suspicions creep into *our* minds, and affect *our* judgments. Riddell storms out rather than face two A10 men. You immediately assume he's crazy, but it could be simply that he's furiously angry. He damages a car belting out of his garage. That isn't necessarily evidence of recklessness; only that he's made a driving error, not difficult to do on a dark night, with half a hurricane blowing. Finally he rushes into the Yard and draws a revolver from stores. That doesn't have to mean he's intending to blast off at anybody. If he's about to conduct inquiries amongst dangerous suspects, it's only sensible for him to go armed."

"You really mean," said Hobbs dazedly, "that you feel we can discount the combined on-the-spot evidence of Rance, Stephenson and Mrs. Riddell, who are all convinced that Riddell's out of his mind?"

"How long had Rance and Stephenson seen Tom for? Ten seconds at the most," said Gideon. "And as for Vi Riddell, she's panicking because *Tom is different from his usual self.* Well, good heavens, who wouldn't be different from their usual selves if they knew that the whole country was maligning them? The Underworld's even found a new name for police brutality – 'doing a Riddell'.

"If I were in Tom's shoes, I'd have an overwhelming urge to get away on my own and somehow prove to the world that I wasn't what I'd been painted. Riddell's only way of doing that is to tackle Stannet and his cronies, and somehow get fresh evidence to reopen the case against them. And that's what I believe he's doing. He's taken on an impossible task, of course, and he must be totally desperate to do it. As a matter of fact, when I saw Tom myself three hours ago, I got the impression that – beneath the surface – he was close to that kind of desperation. But there's a hell of a difference between being desperate and being dangerous. And the simple truth is that Tom's too good a cop to have crossed that line. No matter what his condition – or what the temptation – I'd stake my career on the fact that he'd always stop at murder."

The wind sounded louder, despite the double glazing.

Penny and Kate looked as though they wanted to applaud him.

Alec's face was so stony that it seemed stunned.

"We do *nothing*, then, about Riddell?"

Gideon stopped fingering the bowl of that pipe. He had made his decision. The need now was to stand by it.

"Absolutely nothing," he said very firmly, and then admitted softly: "Though God knows, it's going to be the hardest thing in the world to do."

If only, he thought, he could have just one glimpse into the tormented mind of Tom Riddell.

* * *

Not that, at that particular moment, Riddell's mind was in a very tormented state.

He was sitting on a plain wooden bed in a small room on the top floor of a cheap hotel in Bayswater, feeling rather pleased with himself.

He had gone there immediately on leaving Scotland Yard, signing in under the name of Terry Randall. No questions had been asked about him not having any luggage. He had simply been required to settle his bill in advance: £15 for bed and breakfast, very reasonable as prices went, now that London had become the most expensive city in the world. He had been able to pay the bill easily, and still had £76 in his wallet, and exactly £4.28½ in his pockets in small change.

Riddell knew that, because he had spread all the money out on the little wooden bedside table.

Beside it, he'd put his diary, his notebook, two ballpens, a comb, a box of matches, a penknife, a clip of cartridges and an unloaded revolver: all the contents of his pockets in fact.

He needed to have these things in front of him because every so often there was a buzzing in his head, which made him forget who he was, and why he was here.

But the last time the buzzing had come had been an hour ago, and he didn't think it would happen again tonight.

He was feeling too tired. Deliciously tired. In a couple of seconds he'd take his coat off, flop down on that bed, and be dead to the world.

All he had to do before that happened was just impress on his mind the main facts of the situation again.

You're Chief Detective Superintendent Tom Riddell, he told himself. *You walked out on your home because men from A10 were going to ask impertinent questions. Suddenly you saw the light and realised that staying around and answering them wasn't going to solve anything. That in this sick country, there was only one way to get justice done. Only one way . . .*

"What way?" wondered Riddell sleepily. He groped around in his mind for the answer, and it came, not in words but in actions.

Suddenly he found himself holding the revolver. A moment later, he drifted off to sleep still fondling it. And for the rest of the night, whenever the sound of the gale outside half-awakened him, he would soothe himself by clicking back the safety-catch and pressing the trigger.

*   *   *

Less than half a mile away, in his snug little Bayswater flat, Matt Honiwell would have given a great deal to be able to drift off to sleep.

All he could do was toss and turn, and listen to the wind, which was now making an incessant moaning, uncannily like the sobs of Rita Haig when she first learned about Lenny's death.

As if that memory wasn't disturbing enough, thoughts of that thick, threatening voice on the phone kept coming back, robbing him of all peace of mind, all possibility of sleep.

Well, it's not enough, copper . . . You'll have to do a lot more than that to keep your nose clean and your name out of the papers . . . Just a word to the wise, copper. Just a word to the –

Matt groaned and sat up, his hands behind his neck, staring into the darkness of the bedroom: a total darkness, which seemed symbolic of his future as a policeman.

And yet Netta had been right.

He *couldn't* just resign and let everything he'd worked for be wiped out by a lot of blackmailing murderers.

Somehow he had to find a way of fighting back.

But what way was there? They'd got that bloody cheque, they'd got hard evidence of "bribery and corruption" as the defence would call it, they'd got . . .

"Tell George about it, darling. He'll know what to do."

Netta's anxious, pleading words rang through his head with such clarity that Matt gave a violent start: it was exactly as if she'd spoken them aloud. He peered down at her as she lay beside him, and listened carefully to her deep, regular breathing. Yes, she was asleep all right. And yet . . .

As he stared, she turned over with a sound that was half a sigh, half a groan of anguish.

"Tell George about it, darling, *please,*" she pleaded desperately, and he suddenly realised that she was saying it in her sleep, perhaps to herself, perhaps to an image of a worried Matt whom she was seeing in her dreams.

Suddenly he grinned.

"Don't worry, pet," he whispered gently in her ear. "First thing in the morning, that's exactly what I'll do."

She didn't wake up; but evidently the message got through to her.

Perhaps the dream Matt was saying it to her, taking his cue from the real one.

At all events, she turned over once again, and evidently the nightmare was over. The sound she made this time was a sigh of depthless, almost ecstatic relief.

"I'm so glad, darling. George will take care of everything . . . all our worries . . . you'll see . . . "

"I hope you're right," said Matt dourly. "Personally I'm by no means so cer — "

But something of her relief had communicated itself to his own mind. Enough, anyway, to relax his tension and let his tiredness break through and overwhelm him.

Before he'd finished the sentence, Matt, too, was asleep.

* * *

While the Honiwells were sleepily and thankfully thinking of Gideon as a saviour, nine miles away, in a flashy riverside bungalow near Richmond, John Farrant was roundly cursing him.

"The man's as innocent as a new-born babe. He has absolutely no business at all to be running a tough modern crime-fighting outfit like the C.I.D.," he said.

He was lighting his fortieth cigarette of the evening, and pouring his eleventh or twelfth whisky.

It was past two o'clock but, tired as he was, he had no intention of going to bed until all that whisky had done its work and he could barely lurch there.

His wife Jill — a fluffy blonde with a hard look that became harder whenever she glanced her husband's way — had been keeping pace with John's drinking, but in vodkas rather than whiskies. She was in a silly, giggling mood — and a reckless one.

"I bet you wish you had Gideon in some nice dark interrogation room," she said, and added scornfully: "With, of course, about ten detective sergeants holding him down."

Farrant looked as if he was going to hit her. Jill decided that she wouldn't mind all that much if he did. At least it would mean that he felt some kind of passion for her, and that for once she hadn't been brushed aside by the cold, inhuman force of his ambition.

"You little — "

Whatever unpleasant epithet was coming, Farrant thought

better of it, and broke off with a shrug. He swallowed his current glass of whisky at a gulp, and crossing the room unsteadily, poured himself another.

"God, you'll never understand, will you? I'm not a brute, for Chrissake – don't *enjoy* hitting my fellow human beings about. Half the time, I feel sorry for the poor sods, even when I'm doing it. But you simply can't fight today's villains with yesterday's kid gloves. Show me the page in the Queensberry Rules where it tells you how to deal with a 'kick-to-kill' yobbo, for a start."

"Timothy Dane wasn't a 'kick-to-kill' yobbo, was he?" Jill said levelly.

"No, love." Farrant became heavily sardonic. "Just a friendly neighbourhood arsonist who has killed three firemen, and seriously injured more than twenty passers-by.

" 'An eye for an eye', the Bible says. Well, all I did was give him two or three very slight bruises, in return for all those people his firework displays had maimed and killed. To hear that flaming doctor go on, you'd think I'd got the thumbscrews out and put him on the bloody rack."

He flung himself into an armchair.

"If it wasn't for that f----- Mr. Plaster Saint Gideon, there wouldn't have been any medical report at this stage."

"Then it doesn't sound to me," said Jill, "as if he *is* quite as innocent as a babe."

Farrant grunted.

"Mind you, they still can't *prove* anything against me. Dane's an alcoholic. He's been living rough and sleeping rough. He's been stumbling and falling, even in his cell. He could have got those bruises a million ways."

Jill took one more sip of vodka, and then asked one more question.

"Do you really think that a man like that can *possibly* be Dante?"

Farrant started so violently that he dropped his glass on the floor. Then he lurched towards her.

"You bloody slut, do you think I'd have knocked him about

81

unless – unless I *was* sure? It'd serve you right if I give you some of – of what I gave him.''

"That's just the whisky talking," Jill said provocatively. "And that's just the whisky *walking*," she added, as he swayed and staggered after her around the room.

Long before he could catch her, he had dropped senseless on to the carpet.

His alcoholic snores mingled with Jill's uncontrollable giggles. And the wind outside the bungalow seemed to be joining in with shrieks of hysterical laughter.

*　　　*　　　*

In a cell at the back of Down Lane police station, Timothy Dane was having the roughest night of all.

Nothing alcoholic had touched his lips for more than twelve hours, and every nerve and fibre in his body felt weak and raw from the lack of it. Those bruises kept him wakeful too, making it difficult for him to lie comfortably in any position.

More troubling than anything else were the incessant questions pounding in his head, questions he'd been asked over and over again that day.

Why was he always hanging round paint and chemical factories?

He wasn't sure; he only knew that they fascinated him. After all, he'd been in chemical research, and just by looking through the gates of a factory he could tell what new equipment had been installed there; what fresh developments there'd been in the past few months.

Why had he so often been seen in the very areas where Dante fires were later started?

Again, he didn't know the answer. He hated and dreaded the very thought of fires, but he couldn't escape them; they followed him everywhere.

How could they follow him, if he didn't start them himself?

It was a difficult question, Dane admitted, in his grave, pedantic style. And it led to a still more difficult one.

With all the haziness in his mind, and gaps in his memory, how could he be sure he WASN'T Dante?

Timothy Dane groaned, turned over for the hundredth time, and ordered his brain to stop thinking.

It obliged, enabling him to spend the rest of the night just lying and listening to the wind, as it whistled and roared its contempt at all things human, especially such trivial things as questions and answers.

*   *   *

For one man – a solitary figure standing on a rise near Wimbledon Common, exulting in the gale lashing round him – this rough, wild night was an occasion for the deepest joy.

If only it was like this again tomorrow ... and if only the fireman's strike materialised at midnight tomorrow night ... why, the flames from one or two "spectaculars" would spread like a forest fire.

Turning the whole of London, Dante told himself gleefully, into one vast, unquenchable inferno.

10 Dangerous Day

Next morning, the wind had dropped to below gale force; but it was squally, and strong enough to give a most curious look to the London skyline. The Houses of Parliament, Big Ben, the severe high-rise office block that was the *new* New Scotland Yard – all reared up, dark and drained of colour, against a background of unrelieved grey, across which, much closer to the ground and not much higher up than the old wartime barrage balloons, little squat black clouds kept scudding, at a great rate and in endless procession. It was almost as though some unknown enemy force was maintaining a constant bombardment, silent, sinister, purposeless and yet loaded with mysterious menace. One only had to glance up to get the eerie feeling that something strange and awesome was portended; to feel instinctively that this was a dangerous day.

Gideon, though, did not need to look up to have an awareness of danger. Deeply disturbing problems confronted him almost from the moment of waking. The papers, scanned over his morning tea, were spiky with black headlines about the Stannet verdict. The eight o'clock news on the radio, heard in the kitchen above the sizzling sound as Kate fried bacon and eggs, was largely devoted to the threatened fire-brigade strike. One more meeting between the firemen's leaders and the management was arranged for ten o'clock. If it ended in deadlock, then not a single fireman or fire-engine in the Metropolis would be functioning after twelve midnight. A man "charged with wholesale arson in connection with the Dante case", the newscaster added significantly, would appear before the South London Magistrate's Court at ten thirty a.m.

A stalemate at that fireman's meeting, an awkward magistrate refusing to remand Dane in custody, and London would be facing its greatest fire hazard since 1666, Gideon thought grimly. Then suddenly he realised that there must be some trouble nearer home. Kate had hardly said anything since she'd got up, and although she was setting a sizzling plate of bacon and eggs in front of him, had given herself only a cup of coffee. Either she was worried or slimming, and it had to be worry: slimming wouldn't explain the silence.

"Something on your mind, love?" Gideon asked.

Kate nodded.

"I can't forget about Vi Riddell. I'm dying to ring her to see if she's heard from Tom yet, but don't want to wake her if she's at last getting some sleep."

"Oh, ring her," Gideon said. "For both our sakes! If Tom's contacted her – and sounds all right – it'll be a big load off my mind, too."

But it wasn't the sort of morning on which loads got lightened.

After two minutes' talk with a distraught Vi, Kate was ten times more worried than before.

"She simply hasn't heard a thing since Tom drove off, almost twelve hours ago! She's in a terrible state. She's sure that Tom *would* have rung her, unless – unless – "

She didn't finish the sentence. She didn't have to. Gideon could supply all kinds of endings to it himself, every one of them chilling.

Unless Riddell had met with an accident. Or committed suicide with that revolver. Or gone so crazy that he no longer knew what he was doing . . .

It began to look as if he might have totally underestimated the gravity of Riddell's condition, and in the process made the blunder of his career.

Against the advice of Hobbs, the A10 men, and Tom's own wife, he might have made it possible for Riddell to commit

85

murder.

There were times when Kate could read him like a book, and this was one of them.

She squeezed his arm, and gave him a peck of a kiss on the cheek.

"Don't worry, love. You've stuck your neck out for Tom many times before, and you've never regretted it in the end, have you?"

Gideon was about to point out that Riddell had never *been* like this before. But he changed his mind; Kate was troubled enough already.

"You going over to Vi Riddell's?" he asked; and knowing Kate, already knew the answer.

"Of course. If ever anybody needed a shoulder to cry on, that poor woman does," she said.

Moving with her own special combination of speed and grace, she had got her car out, and was on the way to Wembley a full five minutes before her dazed husband left for the Yard.

* * *

The Riddell problem was still uppermost in Gideon's mind when he arrived to begin his working day; and it was uppermost in other minds, too.

He had been at the Yard barely a quarter of an hour before he was summoned to an emergency conference with Scott-Marle. Also present was what amounted to a deputation from A10: Commander Macgregor supported by Stephenson and Rance. All had discovered the full facts about the Riddell situation. All were demanding to know why no action had been taken about a missing, probably berserk policeman in known possession of a loaded revolver.

Macgregor, a dour Scot with an angular, argumentative-looking face, covered by a mop of prematurely whitened hair, was in his most aggressive mood.

"It's verra hard to resist the conclusion," he finished, "that there are two laws in operation within the Metropolitan police. One law for ordinary policemen – and another for the privileged, cosseted senior men of the C.I.D.! What should we call it – Gideon's Law?"

Gideon could not remember when a jibe had stung him so deeply. Before he realised it, he was on his feet, roaring back: "I freely admit that there *is* a Gideon's Law, and if you like, I'll spell it out for you. It says simply that a policeman has at any rate *some* right to be presumed innocent until he's proved guilty, or to be blunt, presumed good until he's proved bent. I did not consider that there was sufficient evidence last night to suspend Tom Riddell, and then start hounding him down like a wanted criminal. But –" The roar suddenly dropped, and his voice became level, tense, strained. "But the fact that he has now let twelve hours go by without attempting to contact and reassure his wife forces me to conclude that I may have been wrong. The next few hours will tell. They will be very anxious hours, I can assure you, for me."

There was a pause while the implications of all this sank in. Then Chief Superintendent Bob Stephenson – as always, very much a Bobby in his voice and bearing – began quietly: "If I may have permission to speak, sir?" He didn't wait for anyone to give it to him. "Does this mean that Commander Gideon is *still* proposing to take no action about Riddell? Are we just to sit here, twiddling our thumbs, until it's too late and there's been a shooting, perhaps of some entirely innocent –"

To Gideon's surprise and relief, Scott-Marle intervened.

"The Commander's judgment has not yet been *proved* to have been at fault, Superintendent," he said. "On the contrary, I am regretting that I did not listen to him yesterday, when he warned me that an A10 investigation at this stage might lead to disaster."

Faintly smiling, the Commissioner looked Gideon straight in the eye.

"You know your man better than any of us, Commander. Is it still your considered opinion that it's safe to wait for Riddell to make the first move?"

Gideon decided that he could only be completely frank.

"We may have reached a stage where no one's opinion is valid except a psychiatrist's," he said bluntly. "But for what it's worth, sir, I still *feel* that that course is the right one."

A grunt from Stephenson, a snort from Macgregor, and a sharp intake of breath from Jimmy Rance told him that this feeling was not exactly shared.

Scott-Marle ignored them.

"Very well, Commander, I will endorse your decision. This meeting is adjourned," he said quietly.

His manner was correct, impartial, icily aloof; his face, as usual, quite expressionless. But the very immobility of his features betrayed to Gideon that he was really thinking: "God help us all, George, if you are wrong."

* * *

Outdoors and in, the morning grew darker and more menacing.

Gideon returned to his office to find Matt Honiwell waiting to see him: a pale-looking Matt, showing unmistakable evidence of his near-sleepless night, and talking so haltingly that he almost stammered.

"I – don't know how you'll take this, George, but I've b-bungled things badly, and ..." It took him a second to summon up courage to finish the sentence, and then, when the courage came, found himself blurting it out with a rush. "... And I'm afraid the Blackfriars gang has me over a barrel."

He spelt out the details, ending desperately: "With that cheque as evidence of bribery, following what happened to Lenny Haig yesterday, I wouldn't have a leg to stand on, no matter if I caught the whole bloody mob red-handed! If you – if you feel I should be taken off the case – "

Gideon leaned back in the chair behind his desk.

Here we go again, he thought. Another cocky criminal, laughing and jeering like Sid Stannet. Another sincere, dedicated, transparently honest cop looking over his shoulder in terror of suspension and the A10, purely as a punishment for being too conscientious over his job. If it was the last thing he ever did as C.I.D. Commander, he had to halt this trend and bring back simple justice – "Gideon's Law".

The pause dragged on. Matt steeled himself for a withering tirade, or at least, a lecture on letting down the C.I.D.

He could hardly believe it when Gideon suddenly grinned, opened a drawer in his desk and pulled out an expense chit.

"Go downstairs and draw £300 out of the Police Contingency Fund straight away," he said. "That'll turn this 'bribe' of yours into an official Scotland Yard loan, made to the Haig family on compassionate grounds with the full authority and support of the C.I.D. Your cheque was merely an advance, given a few hours early because the Contingency Fund was closed for the night. Does that take care of the blackmail situation?"

The relief on Honiwell's face seemed to light up the room.

"It certainly does, George. It wipes it out completely. I don't know how to thank you."

Gideon's grin faded abruptly.

"You can best thank me," he snapped, "by turning your full attention back to this case. If you hadn't been so preoccupied, you'd have realised that this threatening phone call was a major clue. It points to a far closer tie-up between the Haigs and the Blackfriars mob than you'd supposed. They may even be in cahoots with each other, exchanging information the whole time. It's possible that one of the Haig children is either a member of, or friendly with a member of the Blackfriars mob itself. And if that's the case, you'd be well advised to get men down there, watching the Haigs night and day."

Matt's face fell; and Gideon could guess precisely why.

Honiwell was thinking that he'd done enough to the Haigs, causing the death of Lenny. Now that, in spite of everything, they'd accepted him as a friend, he was very reluctant to start spying on them.

But that was part of the price of being a policeman; a price that Matt, for all his compassionate nature, had never in his career refused to pay.

He was standing now, his normally cuddly features stern and determined.

"I'll send Meadows down to begin with," he said. "He's a bit over-cautious at times, but he's an old hand at this sort of job, and knows how to stay out of sight." The stern look went out of his face; his eyes showed how much he hated himself for doing this. "I — I wouldn't want Rita, or any of the Haigs, to have any suspicion of what was going on."

Poor old Matt, thought Gideon, grinning affectionately at Honiwell's back, as he went out of the door. He was a hopeless softie by today's standards, but in his, Gideon's, book, he was worth a hundred Farrants.

For the first time in a couple of hours, he found his mind turning to Farrant, and all the complexities of the Timothy Dane case. And at that moment, almost as if Fate had arranged it, the door opened and Alec Hobbs came bursting in, with the worst news of that dangerous day.

"I've just had word from the South London Magistrates Court. After only an hour's hearing, it was decided that Dane had no case to answer. He walked out of the courtroom, free as air, more than twenty minutes ago."

Gideon jumped up from his chair.

"Someone's tailing him, I hope," he said sharply. "He simply mustn't be allowed to get away."

"Farrant sent his sergeant after him, I gather. Not the ideal choice — Dane knows him by sight. But there simply wasn't any other plain clothes man in court. And I still haven't told you the worst of it, George. According to the radio, the firemen's talks have just broken down. Which means — "

Hobbs's voice, normally so perfectly controlled, was suddenly husky, as though his throat had gone dry.

"Which means that, if we lose track of Dane, all Londoners can do tonight is pray."

11 No Case

For close on twenty seconds, Gideon stood motionless, alarm, bewilderment and fury battling for supremacy inside him.

Finally, sheer bewilderment won.

The case against Timothy Dane had certainly been a circumstantial one; but how could any magistrate in his right mind have decided that there was no case to answer at all?

For three out of the past four days, Dane had been seen "acting suspiciously", in the classic police phrase, outside Mortimer's Paint factory at Morden. He had signed a statement actually admitting being present at all fifteen of the Dante fires, and his only explanation was that "they seemed to follow him about". He had been a senior research chemist at an explosives factory. He was now an obvious psychopath. And his very name, T. Dane, was an exact anagram of Dante. Surely that was enough, and more, to get anyone remanded pending inquiries, if not actually committed for trial. Unless –

Gideon tensed, as a chilling possibility crossed his mind.

Unless the magistrate had had some reason to suppose that Dane's confession had been faked, or forced out of him under duress.

Unable to keep the grimness out of his voice, he said: "Where's Farrant now?"

"On his way back from the courtroom," answered Hobbs. "Should be here any minute."

"Right. Well, when he arrives, I want him to report to me

91

straight – "

"Here I am, sir," came an interruption from the doorway. "I hope you don't think I've been a naughty boy and blotted my copybook completely."

Gideon glowered. He did not expect his men to tap on the door before they came into his office, but neither did he expect them to come sidling in and rudely interrupt him.

There seemed, in fact, to be no end to the number of ways in which John Farrant irritated him. There he was, lounging against the wall, returning his glower with a look of almost *insolent* innocence.

"Nobody blots his copybook with me until I've heard *his* side of the story, Farrant," Gideon barked. "But I'd very much like to hear your explanation of how a magistrate could possibly have dismissed such a strong *prima facie* case so completely out of hand."

"That's easily answered, sir," said Farrant, suddenly respectful. "Dane had had a bad night – through alcohol deprivation, more than anything, I imagine – and looked white and shaky in the dock. The magistrate asked if he'd had medical attention while in custody."

"As, of course, he *had*, if you'd carried out my orders."

Farrant's air of innocence grew.

"Quite so, sir. He was examined by a doctor yesterday afternoon. The trouble was, that the doctor turned up in court and insisted on testifying. He claimed that Dane's body was covered in bruises."

"Oh, it was, was it?" said Gideon, dangerously quietly.

Ignoring the interruption, Farrant raced on.

"I pointed out that those bruises were to be expected in a man who was in a permanently drunk condition and had staggered and fallen about from the moment he arrived in his cell, but the magistrate, influenced no doubt by the headlines in the papers this morning, came to the conclusion that I'd been conducting a bullying interrogation – in other words, 'doing a Riddell'."

Cunning, thought Gideon. Very, very cunning ... Farrant had deliberately picked that emotionally loaded phrase to bring home how preposterously unjust such charges against C.I.D. men could be. And the point about Dane's drunken state was a fair one. It couldn't possibly be *proved* that those bruises had been inflicted during questioning. If Farrant flatly denied hitting Dane, then under his own principles – under what he'd called "Gideon's Law" – he'd be forced, once again, to let the matter go.

Farrant was making that denial now, with such hypocritical blandness that it was all Gideon could do not to inflict a few bruises himself, there and then.

"I need hardly add, sir," he was saying, "that in point of fact I never so much as *touched* Timothy Dane during that questioning. It would have been as much as my job was worth, wouldn't it, after the specific warning you'd given me earlier in the day."

Gideon took a very, very deep breath, and then, with a jerk of his head, signalled Alec to leave the room. He never dressed a senior man down in the presence of anyone else, even his Deputy Commander.

Hobbs made a quick pretence of gathering up some papers, and then went out. As the door closed behind him, Gideon said, quietly and deliberately:

"Your story did not cut much ice with the magistrate, Farrant, and I don't know why the hell you thought it would fare better with me. I'm not remotely happy with your explanation of those bruises, but you've been clever, and there's no proof against you. All through my career, I have been very reluctant to recommend a man for suspension, and I have never done so unless his guilt was – as the barristers put it – 'beyond all reasonable doubt'. I am bound to tell you that in your case, there is getting to be less and less room left for that reasonable doubt. But as long as there is any at all, I'll give you the benefit of it. Just so long, and no longer. Do we understand each other?"

Farrant turned white with anger. For a moment, his basic contempt for softness and scruples showed in his face, in a look which said plainly: "You and I will never understand each other in a thousand years."

But he recovered rapidly, and within a couple of seconds, was his old cunning, ambitious, hungry-for-praise self.

"I'm quite confident, sir, that by the time this case is over, your doubts about me will have disappeared once and for all."

"Oh, will they?" said Gideon. "For a start, you seem to have bungled badly over Dane's release from the courtroom. Knowing that the magistrate might suspect the evidence, you should have prepared for that contingency. As it is, you've allowed a highly dangerous suspect to walk free with just one C.I.D. man on his tail—a C.I.D. man he already knows by sight! If he gives him the slip, we're in real trouble. Don't forget that Dane has been living and sleeping rough all over the South London area for weeks. He must know dozens of odd corners and cubby-holes that we wouldn't find in a month of house-to-house searching. And in one of those corners, if he really is Dante, he has a stock of highly sophisticated fire-raising devices, amounting to actual incendiary bombs, some of them. He's only got to toss one of those at the right moment over the right wall, and there'll be a blaze that the Green Goddesses couldn't control or contain; and given another gale like last night's, God knows where that would end!"

Gideon's mind flashed back fifteen years, to the last occasion when a fire-raiser had menaced all London. He had spent a whole night directing operations against him—and Kate had never quite forgiven him, because it was on that night that one of their children had died: died when he had been away from home. Ever since then, Gideon had had a special dread of arson cases, and this showed signs of being the worst even he had ever known. That mad fire-raiser, years ago, had had only petrol to play with, not the sophisticated chemicals in Dante's armoury; and in those far-off days, a fire-brigade strike would have been unthinkable. Was it just that he was getting on, Gideon wondered, or was the world really becoming madder, darker, more dangerous year by year?

Farrant was talking hard and fast now, making more lame excuses, probably. Gideon found it hard to concentrate on what he was saying.

94

"I haven't only put my sergeant on Dane's tail, sir. I have two area cars out combing the district, each with two plain clothes men – "

"Each with two men?" Gideon repeated contemptuously. "Good God, man, don't you realise that this is a unique emergency? You want to get every C.I.D. man you can rustle up into that area straight away. Ten, twelve, twenty – I don't care if it's a whole division! We need to have Dane *surrounded* by hidden watchers, if possible, in minute-by-minute radio contact with their base."

Farrant started making objections.

"But with such a lot of men on the job, surely even a psychopath like Dane would be bound to notice one of them."

"Not if you get down there yourself and see that they're deployed properly," Gideon barked. "If you don't think you could cope, there are plenty of men who'd take over the case from you at the drop of a hat. Piluski, Rollo – "

"I can cope, sir, I assure you," Farrant said hastily. "I am just wondering whether it wouldn't be better to pull Dane in."

"On what charge?" asked Gideon. "Remember, thanks to you, he has no case to answer officially."

"But we can get him into a police station for more questioning."

Gideon groaned.

"My God! Haven't you questioned the poor devil enough?"

Totally unrepentant, Farrant countered: "If he's Dante, he's planning the deaths of hundreds. Can you question a man like that too much?"

Gideon sat down heavily behind his desk.

"Let's not go into all that again," he said. "The point is, you can't hold him for questioning for the duration of the strike, and nothing short of that would make London safe. What we desperately need is hard *evidence* against him."

He leant forward, eyes gleaming, as a sudden realisation struck him.

"But if he really is Dante, he'll be giving us that evidence almost immediately! He'll be desperate to cash in on the fire-brigade strike – to him, it'll be the opportunity of a lifetime – and that's bound to make him head straight towards that hidden laboratory. Provided you keep your watchers well hidden – but near enough to close in from all sides if he shows the slightest sign of slipping away – he should lead you straight to all the evidence you could possibly need! If I were you, I wouldn't stay here talking any longer. I'd be on my way."

"Right, sir. Thank you, sir. I'll be off."

Farrant's eyes were gleaming as eagerly as Gideon's as he walked across to the door. But for a different reason.

So the old fool wanted hard evidence against Dane, did he? In that case, thought Farrant, he knew just where to get it.

Without moving a step out of Scotland Yard.

*   *   *

Dr. Geoffrey Anscombe, the civilian expert in charge of the newly-formed Metropolitan police anti-terrorist laboratory, had a professorial air. This was not surprising. He was in fact a full-scale professor, but had resigned his Chair at a major university because of some obscure but bitter academic quarrel.

Even Gideon could never talk to him for long without feeling that he was back at school again, and that if he didn't watch out, might find himself being given a hundred lines.

In Farrant, who had been a very tough child at a very tough school, Anscombe produced the same feeling, but on an altogether more intense level.

It was all Farrant could do not to shrink back from this embodiment of academic authority. Somehow, though, he managed to give his usual performance of enthusiastic efficiency.

"I've just called in connection with the Dante case, Dr. Anscombe. We think we're on to Dante, and might be making an early arrest, if the evidence is satisfactory."

Anscombe – a portly, grotesquely untidy man in his late fifties, with horn-rimmed spectacles that were for ever sliding down his nose, and clothes that were always messy with dropped cigarette-ash – beamed approvingly.

"Very glad to hear it, very glad indeed," he boomed, and Farrant almost expected him to add: "Go to the top of the class, my boy." Instead he asked: "In what way can the Lab. help you?"

"We are hoping to find Dante's secret laboratory, the hideout where he keeps his incendiary devices," Farrant said. "But I'm not quite sure if I could recognise it when I saw it, and I wondered if you could tell me what to look for."

"Ah! Well! Yes! Of course!" Anscombe did not so much talk as ejaculate, once his interest was aroused. "Just come this way."

He led Farrant to a table in the corner, on which several phials and a number of scarred metallic fragments were arrayed. Each fragment was carefully labelled. A typical label read: "Conflagration at Progress Pharmaceuticals, Raynes Park, 14 Oct. Section from casing of incendiary device. Analysis: aluminium, showing traces of potash, magnesium, saltpetre . . ."

A number of other chemicals were listed, with long names in writing that Farrant could not begin to decipher.

"We have relics here from all fifteen of Mr. Dante's little infernos," Anscombe said. "And we believe we've traced the incendiary device behind each one."

"Does he use the same device each time?"

"By no means. At Raynes Park, for example, he left a suitcase just inside the main gate, with a powerful explosive charge set off by a timer. At Fanshawe Paints, Mitcham, back in August, he tossed what you might call a glorified Molotov cocktail over the wall, a simple jar containing a liquid with some of the active constituents of napalm . . ."

"I see," said Farrant. "So what we've got to watch out for is a collection of bomb-shaped metal cases and jars, together with phials or bottles of chemicals. Am I right?"

"Absolutely! You've hit it precisely!"

Farrant's eyes narrowed imperceptibly.

"Any special powders?"

"Ah, yes!" Anscombe took the stopper off a phial, and poured out a little pyramid of what looked like greeny-grey ash on the table top. "If you come across any of *this* lethal-looking stuff – on the floor, on clothing, anywhere – you can be ab-

97

solutely certain that Mr. Dante is in the offing. It's a mixture of common saltpetre and potash with one or two chemicals that have never previously been used by any arsonist anywhere. Once ignited, just an ounce could turn St. Paul's Cathedral into a bonfire."

"Could you give me a small-scale demonstration?" Farrant asked.

"Of course! By all means! Delighted!"

Anscombe turned, and for a moment, was busy hauling a large metal container down from a high shelf several feet away. Farrant seized the opportunity to scoop a little of the grey-green powder into an envelope, and stuff it into his pocket.

A few minutes later – having watched, and been suitably impressed, by the spectacle of that pyramid of powder dissolving into a vivid sheet of flame – Farrant walked out of the laboratory, secretly triumphant.

Despite its bad beginning, nothing could now stop the Dante case from becoming the biggest success of his, John Farrant's, career.

Once a few grains of that powder were "found" on Timothy Dane's clothing, on his hair, or – best of all – between his fingernails, how could any magistrate claim that he had no case to answer?

*   *   *

Farrant had picked the wrong moment to go to the anti-terrorist laboratory.

While he was away from his desk, an urgent telephone call came in for him; and since he had not told the switchboard where he would be, the call was put through to Gideon's office. Normally, Alec Hobbs would have answered, but he was busy on another line; and so it was one of the three telephones on Gideon's desk that finally rang.

And it was to the Commander of the C.I.D. himself that the unfortunate Detective Sergeant Baker had to stutter out the news that Timothy Dane, whom he was tailing, had doubled back down a side-alley in Wimbledon, and got clean away.

12   Storm Warnings

All through the afternoon of that dangerous day, the wind kept freshening, sending the squat, low clouds scudding faster and faster across the sky, and threatening a night of even wilder gales. Storm cones were hoisted round all the coasts. A "batten-down-the-hatches" mood pervaded the whole of London, although, to begin with, only a handful of people knew the terrifying truth: that, if the fire-brigade strike went ahead and Dante remained at large, the city faced a night as perilous as any in its history.

Four men who did know it remained in urgent conference for hours, and emerged with looks as grey as the sky.

Gideon and Hobbs had gone straight to Scott-Marle with the news from Detective Sergeant Baker; and after listening for a few moments, Sir Reginald had called in Crawford, the head of Uniform. This was the branch that would have to carry the brunt of the arrangements for coping with the barely thinkable and almost totally unforeseeable emergencies that might arise if all South London became a series of Dante infernos, with a south-west gale blowing the fires steadily Northwards at eighty to ninety miles an hour.

The most stringent preventive measures were set in hand, of course. One of the most intensive manhunts in London history – involving more than 7,000 men, both Uniform and C.I.D. – was mounted around Wimbledon. Its object was no longer to spy on Dane, but to bring him in at all costs. But he had scuttled away – presumably to what Gideon had called an "odd corner or cubby-hole", and not a trace of him could be found.

At Scotland Yard, wall-size maps of the whole Wimbledon-to-Catford industrial area were pinned up; every Dante-type target factory was earmarked, with arrangements made for massive security patrols. Sums were done to discover how many men these would require; heads shook as it was discovered that, even with all overnight leave cancelled, total coverage of all danger-points could not be attempted, let alone guaranteed. The army units on standby with the Green Goddesses were contacted, and warned what horrific duties might be expected of them. The London Fire Brigade was approached, and asked to send experts on fighting chemical fires to instruct special flying squads of Green Goddess men. The reply came that they had to contact their Union for permission to carry out what might be considered a piece of blacklegging.

It was at that point that Gideon lost his temper.

"For God's sake," he thundered down the phone to some terrified brigade official, "don't you realise that this could be one of the gravest emergenicies that London has ever faced?"

"*I* realise it," the official stammered. "But you can hardly expect the Union to see the matter in quite that light."

"Why not?" growled Gideon. "Haven't they got homes that could burn down, too?"

"Mr. Gideon," the official said. "You *must* understand how suspicious this whole thing looks to the Union. They are convinced it is a bogus scare, got up by the Home Office with police connivance, to hoodwink them into calling off their strike at the eleventh hour. In fact, they're planning a mass meeting in Wembley at eight o'clock, partly to vote on the strike, but mostly to counter what they describe as 'unscrupulous police scaremongering' and to warn all their members against co-operating in any way."

"A mass meeting, eh!" said Gideon. "Do you imagine I'd be welcome if I came to present the Metropolitan police's case?"

"I imagine they'd allow you there, Mr. Gideon, if you made

arrangements with the platform committee. But – er – I think a welcome would be too much to expect, to put it mildly."

"That wouldn't worry me. I'll tell them to throw their rotton eggs while they can – before Dante boils them, and their stupid heads too," said Gideon.

And before the official could say another word, he had slammed down the phone.

One thing had become clear, at least. With a massive manhunt going on in Wimbledon and a stormy mass meeting scheduled for Wembley, the public could not be kept in the dark any longer about the Dante situation. The rumours that would spread could cause more panic than any official announcement.

With the help of Scott-Marle, Crawford and Hobbs, he worded a blunt statement to be released immediately to the press, radio and T.V.

". . . While every effort is being made to capture the criminal known as Dante," the message ended, *"and while an arrest can be expected hourly, it would be folly to deny that, in the meantime, the city is facing a unique and unprecedented hazard. We appeal to everyone to keep calm, and to the London Fire Brigade not to stand idly by and place the lives and homes of thousands at needless risk."*

Sir Reginald smiled wryly.

"I doubt if the Fire Brigade Union would describe that as an unprejudiced statement," he said.

"To blazes with the Union," growled Gideon. And added, under his breath: "Or else it could mean to blazes with us all."

*   *   *

Not all the storms brewing round London that afternoon concerned either the Dante threat or the weather.

At the Haigs' garage in Aldgate, something unmistakably ugly was pending. A long procession of tough-looking East Enders had gone striding angrily through the garage forecourt, and up to the front door of the Haig family's flat. Some of them had been invited in; most had only stopped for a few minutes' conversation with Rita Haig on the doorstep. It was what they did after that that fascinated Detective Sergeant Meadows, the C.I.D. man whom Matt Honiwell had sent to keep watch on the Haigs. They showed no signs of going away, but hung about in the forecourt, their coat collars turned up against the driving wind, their faces grim beneath the darkening skies, grim with sullen rage and hate.

Dick Meadows was a tough, grizzly-haired old campaigner, who would have risen much further in the force if he hadn't had a tendency to be an "old soldier" too, and play for comfort and safety rather than success. Typically, he had picked a vantage-point that was not only out of sight but well out of the wind: a spot on the far side of a telephone kiosk conveniently stationed about ten yards past the Haig garage, on the opposite side of the road. This spot had other advantages. It was close to a café into which Meadows could nip for a cup of tea; and the kiosk itself would provide a ready means of getting in touch with Matt Honiwell at the Yard if some special contingency arose. There was only one drawback: the noise of traffic streaming up and down made it impossible for him to catch a word that the men in the forecourt were saying, and he could only guess at the reason for their strange, sullen anger.

Other detective sergeants might have taken a chance and crossed the road; but Meadows was not too anxious to move from his safe, out-of-the-wind position.

And then suddenly, he didn't have to.

They started chanting – softly at first, but then louder and louder until the sound, blown by the wind, came clear through the roar of the traffic.

"Haig, Haig. Who killed Lenny Haig? Haig, Haig. Who kill-ed Lenny – "

A gale force gust, coupled with a roar from a passing red double-decker, drowned the end of the question. But nothing could drown the answer, roared with a frightening, full-throated fury.

"The Fuzz! The Fuzz! The f------, murdering FUZZ!"

Meadows decided it was time to report to Honiwell. He slipped into the call-box and was about to dial the Yard – but then he realised that the box had been vandalised. The phone's wires had been yanked away from the wall. The damage didn't show from outside the box, which was why he hadn't spotted it before.

His heart beating fast, Meadows left the kiosk, ducked into the café, and asked if he could phone from there.

But the proprietor regretted that *his* phone was out of order, too; and although he was very polite about it, a certain shifty expression in his eyes told Meadows that he was lying.

For the first time in a good many years of steady, playing-safe police work, Detective Sergeant Meadows was beginning to be seriously alarmed.

Like everyone in this street, the proprietor had probably been a friend of Lenny Haig, and sympathised with the demonstration going on across the road.

If he'd been watching him watch the garage, and realised he was from the C.I.D. . . .

"The Fuzz! The Fuzz! The f------, murdering FUZZ!"

The chant was so loud now that it was almost deafening.

Meadows, turned, startled, to find the demonstrators streaming into the café all round him, their faces, in close-up, harder and angrier than ever.

His heart was pounding so fiercely now that it was hard to get his breath.

It only wanted one whisper from the proprietor, he knew, and all that fury would be turned on him.

And then suddenly he realised that it *was* turning on him – without the proprietor having said a word.

*   *   *

On the opposite side of Central London from Aldgate, in a fashionable mews near Park Lane, Mayfair, stood a telephone kiosk that had never once been vandalised. Its freshly-painted interior was so spick and span that it looked as if a chambermaid from the nearby Dorchester Hotel came over every day and dusted it. Even the little mirror set at face-height above the phone gleamed as if it had recently been highly polished.

103

Riddell could hardly bare to look at his reflection in it. It showed every detail of his gaunt, unshaven features; and he found himself being half-frightened, half-hypnotised by his own eyes.

They were a stranger's eyes: wild, red-rimmed and staring. The sight of them started that stabbing pain and buzzing in his head; and suddenly he had to go through that ritual of reminding himself who he was and what he was doing.

"You are Chief Detective Superintendent Tom Riddell. You are here to – to ring your wife whom you must have worried sick, you callous – "

He groped in his pocket, found ten pence, and the next moment was trying to dial his home number. Sheer panic seized him when he found he couldn't remember even this, the most familiar number in the world. Fortunately it was at the beginning of his police notebook, under the sinister sentence: *"In case of emergency, contact next of kin at . . ."*

A moment later, he was listening to Vi's anxious: "Hullo."

She was frightened, of course; terrified that this call might be bringing bad news of *him*.

He tried to speak, but for a second, not a word would come.

"Hullo," said Vi again. "Hullo. Who *is* it, please?" Then suddenly, with the urgency of desperate hope, she added: "Tom, Tom . . . is that you?"

"Yes, love, it's me," Riddell managed to whisper. "Just wanted to tell you I'm all right. Not to worry. Be ho – be home soon . . ."

"Tom!"

It was not so much a shout as a positive scream of joy. And then Riddell could hear Vi yelling the news to someone else, someone called Kate . . .

Oh, Lord, Gideon's wife, he thought. He'd have to be careful. If he gave Vi the slightest clue as to where he was and what he was doing, it would go straight to Gideon via Kate, and a squad car would be despatched to stop him.

And he couldn't trust himself not to give a clue. Not in his present state.

"Yes. I'll be home soon, love," he found himself saying. "Just got a couple of small jobs to do and I'll be home. Tonight ... perhaps tomorrow. Bye for now."

"Bye?" The word came across the wire like the startled cry of a bird. There was always something bird-like about Vi. He could imagine her eyes wide and round as a nestling's as she gasped: "Tom, don't hang up, dear ... For God's sake, don't!"

But Kate would be standing beside her, listening, waiting to report everything to George.

" 'Fraid I must," Riddell said, as gently as he could, and replaced the receiver. There was that buzzing in his head again now; and it seemed to be spreading through his whole body.

For the hundredth time that afternoon, he had to brief himself on the situation.

You are Chief Detective Superintendent Tom Riddell. You've rung your wife ... you now have two jobs to do, the first of them starting immediately.

Suddenly calm again, and almost confident, Riddell stepped out of the phone-box into the mews.

He looked up and down the street, darkening now in the stormy November twilight, but there was nobody about, no one to see him as he crouched behind a low wall, skirting the front garden of the most expensive flat in the mews.

That distinguished barrister, Sir Richard Ainley, would be arriving home any minute now; and as he walked up to his front door, would pass less than a yard from where Riddell was crouching.

Bringing him within point-blank range of that revolver.

*   *   *

Gideon was deeply relieved when Kate rang him with the news that Riddell had contacted Vi.

That confirmed his original belief that there was nothing seriously wrong with Tom. Nothing that merited suspension, or manhunts, or putting the C.I.D. in the humiliating position of providing police protection for arch-enemies of the law like Sir Richard Ainley and Sid Stannet.

105

Be a bloody good job if Tom *was* mad as a hatter and shot them both dead, Gideon thought, jokingly – and the very idea seemed suddenly so preposterous that he turned back to the Dante case, grinning.

The grin soon faded as he thumbed through the pile of reports that had poured in from the "Catch Timothy Dane" operation centred at Wimbledon.

Every street for miles around the town – out as far as Southfields in one direction and Morden in the other – had now been searched several times over, both by area cars and policemen on foot. Raids had been carried out on every known pub, dive, dosshouse and squatters' commune. A constant watch had been kept on Mortimer's Paints, the Morden factory at whose gates Dane had originally been arrested.

But the fact had to be faced: after more than three hours of intense searching and questioning, in broad daylight, by a force of over 7,000 men, not a trace of Dane had been found.

The "drop-out" had really dropped out – of sight, and, it seemed, of existence. Yet how could it possibly have happened?

A man wearing startlingly shabby, even ragged, clothes, to say nothing of his wild face and tangled beard, could hardly walk a hundred yards without someone noticing and remembering him, let alone the four miles he'd have had to have walked to leave the search area.

Certainly, he had enough money to get a bus or train out of Wimbledon; a kindly social worker had given him £10 before he'd been released from custody after the court hearing. But no bus driver in the depot, no ticket collector in the railway – or Underground – station remembered him; and surely they would have done if they'd seen him.

Of course, there remained the possibility that he'd thumbed a lift from a car or lorry. But most drivers are wary of ragged, dirty-looking hitch-hikers. He wouldn't have got a lift without standing at some busy roadside for a good length of time, and again, surely somebody would have seen him.

It seemed much more likely that he had gone to ground locally.

Gideon stared again at the Wimbledon map he had pinned up

on the wall. An "X" marked the back alley where Dane had doubled-back on Sergeant Baker and eluded him.

The alley wasn't in a poor quarter. It ran between some gardens in a middle-class residential area. All around were miles of tree-lined avenues of semi-detached houses, most with garages and sizeable gardens. It was hard to imagine a homeless, friendless drop-out being welcomed into any of them. But was it possible he had underestimated Timothy Dane? What if, down one of those tree-lined streets, behind one of those bright, freshly-painted front doors, he *did* in fact have some kind of a home, some sort of a friend?

Gideon rang Farrant, whom he had reluctantly put in charge of the C.I.D. part of the Wimbledon operation, and suggested a house-to-house search of those residential streets. (Normally, house-to-house searches were in the province of the Uniform branch, but there was no law against the C.I.D. conducting them, and Uniform were already fully-stretched.)

Farrant replied brightly that the same idea had occurred to him, and that he had put just such a search in hand, ten minutes before.

Gideon slammed down the phone with an exasperated grunt. He didn't believe that for a moment. But then, he doubted if he would ever believe a word that Farrant said again.

*　　　*　　　*

A certain Wimbledon householder had, in fact, been "a sort of a friend" to Timothy Dane throughout the past three months. One Christopher Cabot of 67, Palford Gardens had given Dane the run of his house, allowing him to come and go whenever he pleased, dossing down any night he liked in a camp-bed in the corner of the box room. He had even gone further than that, and allowed Dane unrestricted access to his well-stocked drinks cabinet.

Dane had never understood why. All his visits to this house, this haven, this sanctuary had ended with him being in such an alcoholic stupor that the other things that had happened there were just blurs in his memory. He had absolutely no idea that he and his kindly benefactor had spent hours together, talking late into the night; that he had given Cabot precise technical details of how to plan and ignite fires of every sort, and equally precise details of where he, Timothy Dane, spent each day. It had been pathetically easy for Cabot to see to it that his fires "followed" Dane about; and by carefully choosing an anagram of Dane's name for his soubriquet, to make sure that all police suspicion fell on the alcoholic. But it was Cabot who had planned and ignited every blaze.

He didn't look remotely like a pyromaniac. A tall, fatherly man of about sixty, with a soft voice and a self-deprecating smile, he might have been taken for the head of some prosperous family business. But, in fact, he had never married, and lived entirely alone – except when entertaining his invaluable guest.

Dane had arrived at No. 67 less than five minutes after giving Detective Sergeant Baker the slip. He rang the doorbell, but no one answered. His friend, as he always thought of him (Cabot had never told him his name) was evidently out. This did not worry Timothy. He knew where the front door key was hidden: under a loose bit of crazy paving, a yard back from the porch. He stooped, fumbled, found the key, and a moment later was in the hall. He needed no telling where to go next. The drinks cabinet was in the front room, first door on the right ...

By the time Cabot returned home from work at six p.m. (just the moment when Gideon was ordering a house-to-house search of that very area), he found Dane laid out on the front-room floor, absolutely dead to the world and snoring, with an over-turned bottle of whisky lying on the carpet beside him. A slight brown stain on the carpet near the neck of the bottle told Cabot that not *quite* all the whisky had gone into Dane's stomach. But the slightness of the stain suggested that a good eighty per cent of it had.

Folding his arms and smiling his fatherly smile, Cabot gave a little grunt of satisfaction.

"That should keep you out of harm's way for a while, my lad," he murmured.

Showing surprising strength for a man of his years, he lifted

108

Dane up bodily, carried him up the stairs, and deposited him on the camp-bed in the box room. Then, whistling cheerfully to himself, he climbed more steps — this time ladder-like ones — into the loft of No. 67, which was rigged up like a laboratory. Switching on a bare sixty-watt bulb, Cabot ran his eyes over rows of strange, bulb-like objects — objects that would have sent Dr. Anscombe of the Yard's anti-terrorist laboratory into a frenzy. There was enough incendiary material here to send half England up in smoke — or, rather, in a Dante-style spectacular of shattering firebursts and cascading flames.

Christopher Cabot, his eyes gleaming like a miser's in the presence of gold, sat down in front of his incendiary devices and slowly made his choice of the ones he would use tonight, the grand climacteric of his career.

He chose slowly, picking up one device and then another, turning each over and over in his hands, his heart leaping as he saw in his mind's eye the blazing cataclysm that it would unleash.

He had no idea *why* he wanted to fill the world with flames. He had no conscious memory of how it had all begun: how as a four-year-old boy he had had to stand and watch while his drunken father threw all his toys, one by one, into the fire of an old kitchen range, and how his mother had tried to intervene, and had had her face pressed against the blistering top of the stove . . .

He only knew that all his life he had had a fascination with fire: a fascination that had often led him into acts of high courage and daring, but which in recent years had darkened into a secret obsession which now had him totally in its power.

He was still in the loft, still picking and choosing amongst his devices when, two floors below, the front doorbell rang.

He swore softly, and pretended not to hear; but it rang again and again.

Finally, with a weary shrug, Christopher Cabot went downstairs. He opened the front door and peered at the two C.I.D. men standing on his porch. He was left in no doubt who they were. One of them was holding an official search warrant under his nose.

109

"Sorry to trouble you, Mr. Cabot, but —"

"You wish to search this house?"

No trace of alarm showed on Cabot's features. His normally self-deprecating smile merely registered polite surprise.

The leader of the two C.I.D. men burst out laughing.

"Hardly, sir," he said. "We just thought we'd warn you to keep your doors and windows fastened. This Dante is loose in the district, and might try to creep in anywhere."

Cabot drew himself up to his full height.

"If he tries it here, I'll give him a hot reception, I promise you."

"I'll bet you will, sir," the C.I.D. man said. "Good evening ... oh, and good luck at the fire-brigade meeting tonight. I heard on T.V. that you and Commander Gideon are the only people speaking against the strike."

"That's right. And we'll need that luck, believe me, Inspector."

Cabot — better known as Assistant Chief Officer Cabot, second-in-command of the South-East Area of the London Fire Brigade — smiled once more at them before he closed the door.

13 High Risk

"Seven o'clock," groaned Gideon to himself, looking at his watch. In just an hour's time, he was due to speak to the firemen, and he had not made a single note. The reports pouring in from Wimbledon had totally occupied his attention, even though all they had given him was a mounting sense of frustration.

All the efforts of all those men had failed to winkle out one single fact about the possible whereabouts of Timothy Dane.

There was nothing for it, then, but to maintain maximum security throughout the night at all possible Dante targets, regardless of how much it cost in effort and manpower. And a terrifying amount depended on him winning those strikers over to his side tonight.

At least, one speaker had now come forward to support him: a high-ranking fire-brigade officer called Cabot. Gideon believed he remembered the man: a gentle, fatherly character who looked as if he would be happier running a stockbroker's business or a bank, but who had a record of spectacular rescues to his credit almost unequalled in fire-fighting. He wondered what sort of a speaker he'd turn out to be. He hoped he wouldn't become tongue-tied, as so many did when confronted by would-be strikers in a jeering, slogan-chanting mood. He wasn't at all sure that he would come across all that effectively himself. Gideon was well aware that his public image was one of authority. And to an angry trade unionist, authority of any sort

111

meant Management – the *them* who were always trying to put one over on *us*. Gideon loathed the idea of being looked on in that light. But what choice did he have when all London was in jeopardy? The very thought of an inexperienced army unit trying to fight back a Dante inferno made him grab pencil and paper, and start struggling to find something effective to say.

For once, though, words simply would not come. It was almost as if his subconscious was telling him that he was thinking along entirely the wrong lines, and was refusing to collaborate in any way.

Perhaps he'd do better if he tried to dictate his thoughts instead of scribbling them down. And he was sure he'd do better with a ham sandwich and a cup of coffee inside him.

Gideon telephoned down to the canteen for the coffee and sandwiches; then he rang the secretarial department and asked if Sabrina Sale was still in the building. Sabrina, an attractive woman in her early fifties, was the favourite secretary of almost everyone in the top echelons of Scotland Yard. Gideon found her not only attractive but distinctly distracting at times; but perhaps, in his present state, a little distraction wouldn't do any harm. It might even be just what was needed to unglue his brain.

Sabrina and the coffee and sandwiches arrived almost simultaneously.

"Ah, good. So you are still here!" Gideon said to Sabrina, aware that he had rarely made a more inane remark in his life.

"Everyone is still here tonight, Commander," Sabrina replied, with that intriguing smile of hers that might – or might not – be intended to be seductive. "Sir Reginald, Mr. Honiwell, Mr. Hobbs, Commander Macgregor – I can't think of anyone important who's gone home."

Gideon paused, with a sandwich halfway to his mouth. He had been so wrapped up in the Dante case that he had momentarily forgotten how much else was impending on this odd, wild, dangerous night. Matt was obviously still waiting for developments on the Haig case. Macgregor might well be hanging on for news of Riddell. Scott-Marle was probably discussing fire contingency plans with the Home Office. And Alec, like

112

him, Gideon, was basically just standing by, battling against frustration, and hoping desperately for something to happen on any front.

Not, Gideon felt, that anyone would have to do much more waiting.

Dante, the Haigs, Riddell – he had an uneasy presentiment that all three cases were nearing explosion-point, and could blow up in their faces at any moment.

Gideon's sixth sense was very rarely wrong.

The first explosion came before that sandwich had reached his mouth.

The telephone rang in Hobbs's office, and a moment later Alec came rushing in.

"I've had a call I think you ought to take, George. It's that barrister Sir Richard Ainley. He claims – "

Even the normally smooth Alec had to swallow hard before he continued.

" – He claims he's just been murderously assaulted by Riddell."

* * *

Gideon did not wait for Alec to switch the call through. He walked into Hobbs's office, his forgotten sandwich still in his hand, and picked up the receiver.

A moment later, he was listening to the silky voice of the famous barrister, describing his ordeal with that special dramatic flair that could mesmerise even the most hostile jury.

"I returned rather late from the courtroom today, Mr. Gideon. It had been – ah – a difficult case, ending with a discussion in chambers. I did not arrive at my flat until – ah – I suppose about half an hour ago. I garaged my car, as is my usual custom, and then went to the front door. Just as I was about to insert my key in the lock, I heard a rustling in the bushes, and the next second, something was jabbed into the small of my back. Something hard and round. Clearly, the muzzle of a revolver.

"At the same moment, I heard the click of a safety-catch

113

being pressed back, and heavy breathing – the breathing of a madman, I told myself – right in my ear.

" 'Shall I shoot you now, you bastard, or shall we go inside and talk? The choice is yours,' a voice said. It was a voice I recognised as Thomas Riddell's.

"We went inside, into my study. Riddell made me stand facing a bookshelf, with my hands up. Most of the time the revolver was still jabbing painfully in the small of my back.

" 'There's just one thing I want you to tell me,' Riddell said. 'And that's the whereabouts of that skunk Sid Stannet. He's retired to one of his secret addresses, and I just want to know which one. But a word of warning, Sir Richard. If I suspect for one second that you're giving me a spurious answer . . .'

"That was when the most terrifying thing happened. Riddell's voice began to fade out, almost like a radio station going off the air. And I could feel the gun in my back beginning to shake as if he was suffering from a species of epilepsy. And remember, the safety-catch was off . . . Believe me, Mr. Gideon, I honestly feared that that moment might be my last."

This was no longer courtroom drama, Gideon told himself. It was the real thing. Ainley's voice shook slightly itself at the memory of that shaking gun.

"I – ah – have to confess that I told him where Stannet could be reached. It seemed it would be as much as my life was worth not to.

"But Riddell seemed for a moment to be beyond hearing me. The gun went on shaking. It was almost like being on the end of a pneumatic drill. There is no doubt, Mr. Gideon, that he's a very sick and very dangerous man indeed."

It was on the tip of Gideon's tongue to snap: "If so, it was you, Sir Richard, who made him one." But he resisted the temptation. However much Ainley may have deserved the treatment, he had to admit that Riddell had no right, as a police officer, to be handing it out. And he also had to admit that he didn't like this description of Riddell's condition.

Perhaps he had been wrong all along. Perhaps Tom *was* dangerously out of his mind.

Aloud, he said: "What happened then?"

Ainley's voice became steadier.

"I had to repeat the address three or four times before Riddell was capable of taking it in. Then at last he recovered himself, and took the gun out of my back.

" 'Stay just where you are,' he ordered, 'and count to a hundred slowly. Out loud. If you turn round before you've finished counting, it'll be the last thing you ever do.'

"I started counting, and before I'd reached twenty or thirty, he was gone. I made no attempt to pursue him, remembering that gun. I poured myself a stiff drink, and then rang Stannet to warn him that Riddell was on his way."

"Right," said Gideon brusquely. "We'll take it from there, then, Sir Richard, and see that Mr. Stannet has full police protection tonight." Never had the word "Mr." stuck in his throat so much; he felt almost like a pre-war B.B.C. announcer being compelled to say "Herr Hitler".

Ainley gave Stannet's address: The Gables, a large house near Kingston, surrounded by several acres of garden. Gideon had heard of the place; its previous owner, he seemed to remember, had been a rock star. No doubt it was crawling with Stannet's henchmen, and Riddell was in far more danger than his intended victim.

Sir Richard now adopted his most acid courtroom manner.

"I have only one comment to make on all this, Mr. Gideon. It is coming to something when the police have to provide protection against the police."

Gideon was not going to allow that sneer to be the last word.

"And *I* have only one comment to make on all this, Sir Richard," he roared. "It is coming to something when policemen are driven to take such desperate measures to protect themselves against the law."

It was a reckless thing to have said; and Sir Richard seized on it with a barrister's swiftness.

"Am I to take that to mean that, as Commander of the C.I.D., you find Riddell's conduct excusable?"

It was a subtle, deadly question but Sir Richard was not in a courtroom, and the only answer he received was a decisive *burr, burr, burr.*

Gideon had just slammed down the phone.

He had rarely felt so angry, so frustrated in his life.

There was no help for it now: he *had* to order Riddell's suspension. What was worse, he *had* to send men out to this gangster's hideout to arrest Tom as soon as he showed his face, while Stannet and his cronies no doubt stood around chortling.

It would provide a tale the Underworld would be laughing at for years to come. It would represent the total triumph of the bent, the vicious and the criminal against all that he, Gideon, stood for. And it would mean the saddest, most humiliating end conceivable to Tom Riddell's police career.

Yet there was no alternative open to him.

Or *was* there?

Gideon's bitter exasperation faded abruptly as a sudden inspiration dawned.

"You did say that Commander Macgregor was still here, didn't you, Sabrina?" he murmured softly; and without waiting for her to nod, started to dial the number of the Head of Department A10.

*   *   *

The conference in Macgregor's room was a very hurried one, and could not have lasted more than four or five minutes; but it was one of the most dramatic that Gideon had ever attended. And Gideon himself supplied most of the drama.

With Macgregor were the two A10 men on the Riddell case, Jimmy Rance and Bob Stephenson, both of whom had been on their way out of the building when they had been summoned back by an urgent call on the Yard's tannoy system. Beside Gideon sat Alec Hobbs, who kept looking at his watch, as if anxious to get moving.

Gideon began by repeating the gist of Sir Richard Ainley's call. As he finished, he roared: "To misquote someone in the history books, if Riddell's mad, then I wish he would bite some of my other men! Despite his condition – and for all I know, he

116

may be having a complete nervous breakdown – he has already confronted the cleverest and most crooked barrister in England, and forced out of him the secret hideout of London's most vicious gangster."

"Breaking at least a dozen laws in doing so, let's no' be forgetting that," Macgregor said dourly.

"I'm not forgetting it, nor denying that he must be suspended," Gideon snapped. "But that doesn't detract from what he's achieved, and now he's apparently following it up by planning a lone visit to Stannet's hideout, and a direct confrontation with Stannet himself. I don't know about you, gentlemen, but the sheer courage that the man is showing takes my breath away. And whatever state he may be in, he simply does not deserve to be arrested by his own colleagues in full view of his enemies, and dragged off to be dealt with by men in white coats."

"What do you propose, then, Commander?" Macgregor asked, only just keeping a note of derision out of his voice.

Gideon stood up, his massive frame towering over the small boardroom table, effortlessly dominating the room.

"My plan is this. The operation tonight will be led by Deputy Commander Hobbs, accompanied by you, Rance, and you, Stephenson."

"A10 men are to confine themselves to internal investigations," Macgregor snapped, as tonelessly as a robot programmed to repeat only the rule book. "They are not to be employed in C.I.D. work under any circumstances whatsoever."

"I'm not suggesting that they should be," Gideon said. "Their function tonight will be to act purely as observers. As such, they will be doing no more than continuing their investigation of Riddell's fitness to continue as Chief Detective Superintendent. What could be more relevant to that investigation than a chance of seeing their subject in action?"

Macgregor's eyes narrowed.

"It almost sounds as if you expected them to be hidden, watching through spyholes or something."

Gideon smiled.

"That's precisely the idea. If it's explained to him that we need more evidence against Riddell, I am sure that Stannet will have no objection to arranging for both Hobbs and the A10 men to be hidden behind curtains, or in an adjacent room, where they can overhear all that goes on between him and Riddell. Hobbs will of course be ready to intervene if the situation looks as if it might get out of hand. But the danger will be to Riddell rather than anyone else, because Stannet will be bound to have armed bodyguards in plenty on the scene."

Macgregor still hesitated.

"I'm afraid I'm at a loss to see the point of this, Commander. What exactly are you expecting to happen when Riddell meets Stannet?"

"I have no idea," said Gideon. "I only know that it was to arrange this confrontation that Riddell ran out on his wife, evaded Rance and Stephenson here, held up Ainley and very gravely jeopardised his whole career. In view of the length and distinction of that career, I think we owe it to him to let that confrontation happen."

"Even though there is a high risk that he is out of his mind and could well try to shoot Stannet or physically attack him?" Macgregor asked. "Surely by playing it this way, you're almost asking for trouble."

Gideon sat down slowly. His voice was softer, but not a whit less determined, as he answered: "Yes, I am asking – or at any rate, hoping – for trouble. Trouble for Sid Stannet. He's known to be a hysterical type, and there's just a chance that Riddell might succeed in breaking his nerve. And I'd rather *that* happened than that he was left grinning all over his face." Suddenly impassioned, he glared round the room, and ended: "Wouldn't all of you? Or is Riddell the only policeman in London who still believes in fighting criminals, not mollycoddling them?"

No one cared to meet that challenge. The meeting broke up with a startled scraping of chairs, and within minutes Alec Hobbs, Stephenson and Rance, found themselves in a police area car being hurtled towards Kingston, revolvers in their pockets and a great deal of uneasiness in their minds.

Gideon, meanwhile, found himself being hurtled into another

crisis.

The moment he was back in his office, Matt Honiwell burst in.

He had just received news of the anti-police riot that had taken place in the forecourt of the Haig garage in Aldgate, two hours before.

"Two hours?" said Gideon. "Why the hell haven't we heard till now?"

Matt ran a hand through his mop of curly hair. Both the hand and the hair were gleaming oddly, as though damp with sweat.

"The whole street's violently pro-Lenny," he said hoarsely. "Nobody reported it, partly because they sympathised with the rioters, partly because they didn't dare."

"Didn't – *dare*?" Gideon tensed. "Why should they have been so scared?"

He broke off, realising that Matt hadn't told him the whole of it yet. And was having great difficulty getting out the rest.

"Meadows?" he asked softly.

He had a quick mental image of the homely, cautious detective sergeant. And turned cold at the thought of what a mob like that could have done to him.

14   Fire Ahead

Slowly, Matt spelt out just what had happened.

The rioters had seized hold of Meadows, probably in a café across the road, and dragged him to the garage forecourt. There they had kicked him until he was senseless, and were pouring petrol over him, preparatory to turning him into a human torch, when Rita Haig had come rushing out and stopped them.

"How do you know all this?" Gideon asked.

"A passer-by who saw everything finally developed a conscience, and went into Aldgate Pump police station with the whole story.

"After Rita's intervention, the mob chucked Meadows into a second-hand car that was up for sale on the far side of the forecourt, and just left him there, unconscious, bleeding in a dozen places and barely breathing. He was discovered only about a quarter of an hour ago, and rushed to hospital. He's not got a lot of chance of pulling through, but he's alive, and that's something.

"As for the garage, it's been hastily locked up, and the Haigs' flat appears to be empty. The whole family, it seems, have finally had enough and scarpered, and God knows, I don't blame them."

Matt had rarely sounded quite so bitter and weary. His face was a study in self-reproach.

"When I think that I've been sitting here all the bloody afternoon, twiddling my thumbs and waiting for Meadows to make contact! If only I'd sent someone to check on how he was!''

"You had no reason to suppose he'd be in any danger, as long as he kept out of sight," Gideon said. "If this was anyone's fault, it was Meadows's for letting himself be spotted by the gang."

"The gang?"

Gideon groaned.

"Hasn't it dawned on you yet, Matt, that the Blackfriars mob are bound to be behind this whole thing? Whoever heard of an anti-police riot — or any other kind of riot, for that matter — starting in broad daylight, in a damp and windy garage forecourt, at a time when all the pubs have been closed for an hour? The whole thing sounds to me as if it was deliberately staged.''

Matt stared.

"Staged? But what for?"

"As a cover-up for the attack on Meadows, of course." Gideon was suddenly pacing the room. "We know for a fact that the Blackfriars mob, for reasons best known to themselves, *are desperately anxious that the Haig garage should not be watched.* Remember that blackmail call you received last night. Its whole purpose was to induce you to 'lay off the Haigs and give them and their garage a wide berth from now on'. At least that's how you reported the call to me."

"And that's certainly what it said," Matt agreed, marvelling at Gideon's ability to recall the exact words used.

"Right." Gideon moved to the window, and stared down at the stream of traffic moving down nearby Victoria Street. "Well, the blackmail worked, up to a point, and that garage was free from surveillance for the rest of the night. But evidently, that wasn't enough for the Blackfriars mob's purposes. Today, when they spotted Meadows, and realised that you were ignoring their threats and having the place watched after all, they obviously decided they had to remove him at all costs. Staging a riot was the simplest way of doing it without putting any suspicion on themselves. It would look like murder by anonymous members of the public, outraged by the continued police harassment of a family they'd already made fatherless."

121

Matt winced, as fresh memories flooded in of all that had happened the previous day. First Lenny, now Meadows ... Every move he made in this case seemed to end with someone either dead or dying.

Gideon was pacing the room again now, pacing and thinking equally furiously.

"We were working on the theory that it was the *Haigs* the mob didn't want watched," he said. "But we mustn't overlook the fact that it may not be the family at all. After all, one copper across the street can't do all that much spying on a family of seven, especially if they're coming and going all the time! From the speed and ferocity of the way they attacked poor Meadows, I'm inclined to think it must be *the garage itself* that they don't want under observation."

"But why? What can there possibly be about a garage that's so important!"

"Your guess is as good as mine," grunted Gideon. "But it will be a damned sight better than mine when you've got down there and had a look round. If I were you, I'd be on my way. But, Matt—"

Honiwell, nearing the doorway, was spun round like a top by the urgency in those last two words.

"Yes?"

"Take plenty of men with you, and even so, go carefully," Gideon said. "You're dealing with trigger-happy killers in a district which passionately hates the police in general, and—"

Matt smiled bitterly.

"—and one policeman in particular: *me!*" he finished. "Don't worry, George. I'll watch it. Every inch of the way."

*   *   *

It wasn't only Matt who needed to "watch it" tonight, Gideon thought grimly, as the door closed behind Honiwell.

The time was already seven forty. He'd be late for that fire-brigade meeting unless he left right away.

Which meant that he'd only have time to scribble a few rough notes for his speech in the car.

122

A few rough notes, for a speech of such overwhelming importance that his throat ran dry at the thought of it.

For the simple fact was that that speech could well be the only thing that now stood between London and a night of inferno.

*　　　*　　　*

To Dante himself, it seemed that quite a number of things still stood between London and a night of inferno.

There was the fact that South London was crawling with policemen, still carrying on their fruitless search for Timothy Dane.

There was the fact that all-night guards were almost certainly being mounted at all the likeliest paint and chemical factories.

Finally, there was the fact that Gideon – a very powerful, if by no means brilliant speaker, so he'd heard – was more than likely to persuade the firemen to postpone the strike. (Ironically, he would himself be on the platform giving Gideon his support. He simply hadn't been able to resist when the administrative head of the whole South London Fire Brigade had telephoned and asked him to volunteer for the job.)

All these facts together would make it impossible for him to operate effectively tonight.

But they all depended on one thing: Timothy Dane remaining uncaught.

Once Dane was arrested and clapped safely into a prison cell, the whole Metropolitan police force would · say to itself "Emergency Over". The thousands of searching policemen would vanish. The factory patrols would be called off. And Gideon would probably withdraw his plea for a strike postponement.

It was true, of course, that he would no longer be able to use Dane to direct suspicion away from himself. But did that really matter? His very job was the biggest suspicion-distractor conceivable. The very idea of Assistant Chief Officer Cabot, hero of the London Fire Brigade, being Dante would strike most people as too preposterous to be considered; a sick joke almost on the Monty Python level.

Yes, Cabot told himself, he was safe enough.

And his plans for tonight would be safe enough, too, as soon as Timothy Dane was under arrest.

He decided to see to that little detail immediately, on his way to the fire-brigade meeting.

He walked into the box room, and stared down for a moment at the bedraggled figure on the camp-bed. Dane was still deep in alcoholic slumber, snoring loud enough to wake the dead. The sight filled Cabot with loathing and disgust. He didn't know why. The memories of his bullying, drunken father were buried deep beyond conscious recall.

He picked Dane up bodily – he ate so little that he weighed hardly anything – and carried him first downstairs, and then out to his car, a small Citroën.

A moment later, he was driving off in the direction of Wembley, with Dane stretched out on the back seat behind him, no longer snoring now but muttering something into his matted beard.

It sounded like "Don't let him hit me", repeated over and over again.

They were soon in the perfect spot for Cabot's purpose, a quiet back alley only a hundred yards or so from Wimbledon police station.

He pulled the Citroën into the kerb, and stopped. Then he leaned over his shoulder, and opened the back door on the right hand side.

"Timothy," he called gently. "Time for walkies . . ."

Dane woke with a jerk, sat up dazedly and blinked around him. His mind was evidently still grappling with the dream.

"Don't let him hit me . . ."

Cabot chuckled.

"He's not going to hit you, Timothy," he said cheerfully. "But I'm afraid the pavement is."

Using both hands, he seized Dane by the lapels of his battered suit, yanked him up off his seat and hurled him sideways clean out of the car.

As Cabot slammed the door, and the Citroën started to move

away, Dane was scrambling to his feet, rubbing his bruises and calling out bemusedly: "What did you do that to me for? Where am I? What – "

"Just you keep that up, my friend," Cabot chuckled over his shoulder. "It's as good as shouting: 'Here I am! Arrest me!' "

Next moment, the car had turned out of the alley, and Dane had vanished from Cabot's sight – and mind.

In another minute, the Citroën was roaring up the hill, close to Wimbledon Common, which was Cabot's favourite nocturnal haunt. There in the distance stretched the whole vast London skyline, crowned by the Post Office Tower, gleaming as brightly as a candle on a cake.

Dante stopped the car, wound down the window, and laughed as he felt a strong wind fan his face. Not as good as last night's gales, but it was southerly, and so it would do. It would do very well indeed.

He looked at the skyline again, his eyes now gleaming with excitement: an excitement which bordered on ecstacy as his imagination took over, and he saw everything, from the Houses of Parliament to the newest high-rise office block, becoming one vast sea of flame.

With a supreme effort, Dante pulled himself together, and as Assistant Chief Officer Cabot, hurried on towards Wembley.

He arrived at the meeting just in time to walk magisterially on to the platform, side-by-side with the other distinguished guest speaker, Commander Gideon.

*   *   *

Meanwhile, for more than a quarter of an hour, Timothy Dane had been walking, anything but magisterially, up and down that side alley near Wimbledon police station. He could not clear his mind; could not remember how he had got there, what he was doing, where he ought to go.

Suddenly he heard a shout, followed by footsteps, and was momentarily blinded by a torch flashed full in his face.

"Well, well, well, if it isn't Mr. Dante Dane," said a voice which sounded triumphant and gloating.

125

It actually belonged to a Detective Constable Gibson, who had taken this side alley as a short cut home from duty, and was finding it hard to believe his luck.

Dane began feebly to protest that he was not Dante. Or, rather, that he didn't *think* he was Dante. But that cut no ice with Gibson.

"We'll have to see what Chief Detective Superintendent Farrant says about that, won't we?" he shouted jubilantly.

"F-Farrant?"

Even in his confused state, Dane started violently at that name.

And during the hundred-yard walk to the station, he was back to muttering, "Don't let him hit me!" over and over again.

15 Emergency Over?

The fireman's meeting turned out to be the greatest ordeal of its kind that Gideon had ever experienced.

It was held in a large school gymnasium, hurriedly borrowed for the purpose, on the outskirts of Wembley; but the hall was packed so tightly that Gideon had the impression that he was facing a Wembley-stadium-sized crowd – a vast sea of angry faces and waving, blue-uniformed arms, some of them holding banners. "GET OFF OUR BACKS, GIDEON!" said one, and another, still more hurtful, read: "THE WORST CROOKS IN LONDON ARE IN THE C.I.D." Somewhere at the back, surfacing like metallic Loch Ness Monsters from the stormy ocean of furious men, were two T.V. cameras, one from B.B.C. News, the other from I.T.N. So the whole nation was going to see him booed and jeered and told, in that time-honoured Union phrase, to "get on his bike".

Somewhere else in the audience – although he couldn't see them from the platform – were Kate and Vi Riddell. The hall was only along the road from the Riddell's smart little semi-detached home, so Gideon had rung up and suggested they should come, and – with great difficulty – had persuaded the fire-brigade Union to give them seats. "It won't be exactly a Gideon benefit night, love," he'd told Kate, "but it might take Vi's mind off things to come and see me pelted with rotten eggs and tomatoes, and it'll do me a power of good to feel that you're out there, on my side."

"But why should they be so angry with you?" Kate had asked. "You don't care about their silly strike. You're only trying to save lives – and perhaps all London! Can't they see that?"

"They will by the time I've sat down, I promise you," Gideon had said grimly.

But one look around the hall was enough to tell him what a rash promise that had been. Hostility he had expected: men on the brink of striking never take kindly to Management figures counselling caution. But what surprised and dismayed him was their obvious suspicion of the C.I.D., and equally obvious distrust of him as its Commander.

On top of that, came the shaming realisation that that suspicion wasn't limited to this particular audience. These people were just reflecting a feeling that, in the past twenty-four hours, had spread across all Britain.

The Stannet trial, with its multiple allegations against Riddell. The death of Lenny Haig under questioning. The magistrate's complete dismissal of the case against Timothy Dane, after hearing the doctor describe his bruises – all these news items, crashing in on top of one another, had made the whole Metropolitan police force seem like one vast Dirty Tricks Department in the public eye. And all the emergency measures which he, Gideon, had taken that day – the Wimbledon manhunt, the drilling of the Green Goddess teams in chemical fire fighting, the intensive watch on all vulnerable factories – must appear to these firemen to be just so many more dirty tricks: attempts to create a bogus scare, to hoodwink them into calling off their strike.

By the time Gideon was called on to speak, the meeting had already been going on for three-quarters of an hour. The secretary of the Union had reported at length on the breakdown of the talks with the Management: the latest Management offer – of around sixteen per cent – had been greeted with roars of contempt; the sea of angry faces had become a forest of shaking fists. A motion to strike at midnight was proposed and seconded, and it was clear that when the vote was taken, it would be passed by a massive majority.

"But before we *do* put it to the vote," the chairman said, "there are two people on this platform who would like a word with you. First – Mr. George Gideon, the Commander of the C.I.D."

This was greeted with a sound somewhere between a groan and a roar of anger. Keyed up to pass their angry vote, the last thing the strikers wanted was to hear objections, warnings, a call to duty. All of which, thought Gideon grimly, they knew bloody well they were going to get from him.

He stood up slowly, his expression almost Churchillian in its defiance.

"Let's get one thing straight," he said. "I'm not here to hoodwink or bamboozle anybody. I am here simply to state facts – facts which I dislike as much as you do, but which I happen to believe should be *faced*, for the sake of everyone in this room – and for that matter, for the sake of everyone in London."

It was an impressive opening, and was rewarded by an attentive silence.

So far, so good, thought Gideon and, his voice becoming tense and urgent, he went on: "Fact No. 1. At large in this city at the moment is the most dangerous arsonist in the whole history of crime . . ."

That was when the first interruption came.

"What – that poor drunk tramp that the magistrate *let off* this morning?" said a voice from the back, and the hall rocked with laughter. From then onwards, there were derisive jibes after virtually everything Gideon said. When he tried to stress the fearsome consequences that might follow from a spectacular chemical blaze being fought by a handful of army amateurs, a man in the front row shouted: "That's the government's lookout, ain't it? If they want more hoses on the flames, they need to put more money on the flaming table!"

This was greeted by two full minutes of deafening cheering. Then a chirpy shop steward, sitting on the platform committee behind Gideon, capped it all by saying, in a broad stage whisper that must have carried to at least the first fifty rows: "Best sit

129

down, George. It's the only thing to do when you haven't a leg to stand on!''

It was the platform committee's turn to rock with laughter.

Only one face amongst them remained grim; a gentle, fatherly face which Gideon recognised as belonging to Assistant Chief Officer Cabot, the fire-brigade hero who had come to this meeting to support him.

Suddenly Cabot was on his feet, saying, quietly but very distinctly: "I wonder how many of the people in this hall will be laughing in four hours' time, when the whole of London, including your very homes, could be blazing around you!"

Cabot did not sound as if he was visualising a possibility. It was exactly as if he was making a cold, precise prediction. And his voice carried such a curious ring of certainty that the whole audience was stunned into silence.

"I'm sorry I interrupted you, Commander," he whispered to Gideon, with a courteous bow.

"Don't apologise. I'm very glad you did," Gideon whispered back, and wondered why he wasn't feeling as grateful as he pretended; why there were odd, electric tingles travelling all the way from the nape of his neck to the base of his spine. He turned back to the audience, who now seemed at last prepared to listen to everything he had to say.

It took him perhaps ten minutes to outline the whole danger to London; and then he ended dramatically:

"Our inquiries into the Dante case are now proceeding so fast that we confidently expect a final arrest within, at the most, forty-eight hours." (It was a claim so reckless that it almost made him breathless as he said it; but there was no point in suggesting a longer postponement. He would be jeered out into the street if he tried.) "Is it too much to ask you to bear with us for just those two days and nights? It will not affect your chances of winning the dispute in any way. And you could be stopping nothing less than a second Fire of London."

There was no applause when he sat down. But neither were there any jeers or catcalls. There was just a continuation of the thoughtful silence that had started when Cabot had made his chilling interruption. At last, the silence was broken by someone asking to move an amendment to the motion: that the strike should start at midnight, *two days on from now.*

The chairman immediately put the two motions to the meeting.

Quite a large number of hands went up in support of starting at midnight, that very night; but not so many as Gideon had expected.

Then what the chairman called "the Gideon motion" was put to the vote.

Gideon's heart leapt as he saw hands shooting up in every part of the hall. Appearances could be deceptive, but it looked as if he had a clear — if not an overwhelming — majority.

The counting was still going on when a police sergeant came up and whispered in his ear.

"Someone wants to speak to you urgently on the phone, sir. Chief Detective Superintendent Farrant — "

Gideon hurried off the platform, and a minute later, was hearing Farrant's excited announcement of the arrest of Timothy Dane.

"But that's not all, sir." Farrant was almost gabbling. "While talking to Dane, I happened to notice that there was an odd kind of dust on his coat. A powdery dust, almost reminiscent of gunpowder. I took a sample and sent it off at once to the laboratory at the Yard. They have just telephoned back, sir." Farrant paused there for sheer lack of breath. Then he blurted on: "The powder is a rare and highly incendiary substance *used only by Dante.* I think that makes it pretty certain that we've got our man this time, sir, don't you?"

"I certainly do," said Gideon, his own voice hoarse and dazed with relief. "This time, Farrant," he went on warmly, "you've really earned all the congratulations I can give!"

He strode back on the stage to hear the news that the "Gideon motion" had been carried — appropriately, by a majority of 1666, the date of the first Fire of London.

With undisguised delight, he announced to the audience that as far as he was concerned, the motion could now be annulled,

131

and the strike could start as scheduled. Dante had been arrested, *and* positively identified. The emergency was over.

"So now," Gideon ended, surprising the whole audience with a broad, mischievous grin, "it will give me great pleasure to get off your backs and on my bike. Good night!"

This was greeted with a spontaneous burst of cheering that nearly raised the roof. Whatever their feeling about the C.I.D., it was clear that no one in the audience had any longer any distrust of its Commander.

There was only one queasy moment to spoil Gideon's triumph.

Assistant Chief Officer Cabot suddenly got up, came across stage, and proferred his hand.

"My congratulations on the C.I.D.'s achievement, Commander."

Gideon's sixth sense stirred again, filling him with sudden, stabbing doubts. It was almost as if it was trying to tell him that there had been no achievement at all.

*   *   *

Half an hour later, Gideon and Kate were sitting in the Riddells' lounge, both of them trying to calm Vi's near-hysterical worries about Tom.

Gideon had telephoned the Yard, and found that nothing had yet been heard from Hobbs, Rance and Stephenson, all of whom were now presumably at Sid Stannet's mansion hideout at Kingston, awaiting the arrival of Riddell.

Gideon had not told Vi all the facts that he now knew about Tom; but he had assured her that the trouble was nearing its climax, and that it would be over soon.

"We'll know more in an hour or two," he said. "And it could very easily happen that before midnight Tom will be back safe home with you. He'll probably be in an odd state, but nothing that a few days' rest and perhaps a few tablets from the doctor won't put right."

He might be raising false hopes, he knew. Riddell might need weeks in hospital to recover his mental balance. He could be facing criminal charges, and be refused bail. But Vi needed reassurance more than anything in the world; and he was only saying what *could* happen, if all went miraculously well.

Vi, with one of her quick bird-like movements, darted across to him and clutched his arm.

"You're *sure* about that?" she said, her eyes wide and desperate.

Gideon gently removed her hand. He couldn't make false hopes false certainties.

"No," he said quietly. "I'm not sure. None of us are sure of anything about Tom, yet. But for what it's worth, I have a hunch that . . ."

He broke off. Talking of hunches had reminded him of that moment on the stage at the fireman's meeting when he had been filled with strange, stabbing doubts about the Dane arrest.

Those doubts were now back in force.

Overwhelmed with surprise and relief, he had been perfectly sincere in congratulating Farrant; but ought he to have forgotten so completely that Farrant was the most suspect of all the men under his command?

When Farrant had arrested Dane before, it had ended in a humiliating fiasco for him: worse, it had brought him under the shadow of suspicion. And a man of Farrant's mentality would go to any lengths to ensure that next time he encountered Dane, the charges stuck.

To any lengths . . .

Suddenly it dawned on Gideon just how easy it would be for the investigating officer in charge of the Dante case to obtain specimens of that incendiary powder. All he'd have to do was stroll in to the anti-terrorist laboratory and fill an envelope when nobody was looking.

Doubts were not stabbing Gideon any more. They were crashing down on him from all sides, with the force of hailstones. Amongst them was the crushing realisation that Farrant, as head of the C.I.D. contingent in the the Wimbledon manhunt, would now be in full charge of Timothy Dane, because it had been a C.I.D. arrest.

That meant that, at this very moment, he was probably conducting another bullying interrogation.

Christ! He had to stop that at all costs. *Now.*

Hardly noticing Kate and Vi's puzzled stares – and forgetting even to ask permission to use the phone – he shot out of his chair and into the Riddells' hall. He rang Wimbledon police station, and the startled girl on the switchboard, unused to the Gideon roar, switched him through to Farrant with the absolute minimum of delay.

"Hullo again, sir."

Farrant's self-preening air suggested that he was expecting more congratulations. He sounded as taken aback as the switchboard girl when Gideon barked, in a tone as sharp and staccato as a burst from a Sten gun: "Something has just struck me, Farrant, and it ought to have struck you too. After what happened at today's court hearing, there can of course be absolutely no question of you personally interrogating Dane. I hope you haven't started doing so. If you have, you must stop at once."

There was a long pause. When Farrant spoke again, he was almost stuttering.

"But, but surely Dane must be questioned, sir. Who do you suggest should do it?"

Gideon hesitated for just one second; then suddenly he knew there was only one answer he could give.

It was an answer that totally silenced Farrant – and, when it was repeated to them, sent shock waves throughout the whole Wimbledon contingent of the C.I.D.

"Me," said George Gideon simply. "I'll be coming over right away."

16   "Your Friend – Dante"

It was nearly half past ten when Gideon, having left Kate once
again with the distraught Vi Riddell, pulled his large, comfortable Rover to a halt outside Wimbledon police station.

A moment later, he was welcomed – if that was the word – by
an extremely nervous and excitable Farrant, who was being
cocky one moment, and almost obsequious the next.

"I'd like to say, sir, that I think you were quite right to stop
me questioning Dane. After that magistrate's ruling this morning – "

"It would have been a disastrous move for you to make,"
Gideon interrupted. "Right. Well, there's no point in standing
about. Lead me to him."

Farrant hesitated. Gideon noticed that he was visibly
sweating.

"There's just one point I think I ought to stress . . ."

Gideon folded his arms.

"Well, go on, then. Stress it."

"Dane – er – may repeat to you that cock-and-bull story
about me hitting him. The one he told the magistrate – "

"And the doctor substantiated," said Gideon grimly. "Don't
worry, Farrant. I don't go back on my word. Seeing that the
man was an alcoholic, given to falling about, and that his
statements might not be trustworthy, I told you you were getting
the benefit of the doubt over this business. For the very last
time."

"Thank you very much, sir. I just thought I'd – "

"You just thought you'd remind me. Well, you have. Now which way is Dane?"

"I've had him sent to an interrogation room upstairs, sir. It's just this way."

Farrant was suddenly being as smarmy as a head waiter. Gideon's dislike and distrust of him grew with every step they took together along the corridor and up the stairs. When they reached the door of the interrogation room – outside which stood two uniformed constables, who each saluted smartly – Gideon turned to Farrant, and said: "Thank you very much. I think I can carry on on my own now."

Farrant made no move to go: his over-shiny shoes seemed glued to the floor.

"I think I should warn you, sir, that Dane's mind is *very* confused."

Gideon glowered.

"Well, mine isn't," he snapped. "And I don't intend to let it be by him, or you, or anyone else. Do I have to ask you *again* to leave us alone?"

Farrant at last realised that he was beaten.

"I shall be on hand, sir, if you need my help at all," he gabbled, and went off down the stairs so rapidly that he missed a step halfway down, and almost fell headlong.

Nerves, Gideon wondered – or guilt?

He mustn't be too ready to assume the latter, he told himself severely. Farrant was still – just – entitled to the benefit of the doubt.

The constable to the left of the door unlocked it, and held it open for Gideon to go through. The other constable stood by, tense, as though fearing that the prisoner might charge into the corridor.

Gideon was faintly amused by these precautions. Then he remembered that the man inside had been the subject of one of the most dramatic manhunts in London's history, only a couple of hours before. Of course no one here was taking any chances.

He went inside; the door was slammed and locked behind

him, and he was alone with Timothy Dane, the man who stood accused of planning the most terrifying acts in the whole history of arson.

But one glance at the desperately frail, despicably dirty figure shrinking back at his advance was enough to make the whole idea seem absurd.

Gideon's heart missed a beat. Had he really turned half London upside down – expended the energies of 7,000 policemen – simply to land the wrong man? There was one far more alarming thought than that. If Dane was the wrong man, then all London tonight was wide open to the right one . . . And what hope was there of catching *him* now?

Suddenly Gideon was close to despair, and no great distance from desperation.

"Don't hit me," Dane was pleading pitifully. "I'll tell you anything, sign anything you like. Just don't hit me, that's all."

Gideon's despair was suddenly tinged with fury. He needed no telling now why Farrant had been so jittery in the corridor. But – to be fair – it wasn't unknown for men of the vagrant and drop-out type to make false, whining accusations against the police. Once again, he cautioned himself against jumping to conclusions.

Fighting down all these conflicting emotions, he said aloud, as calmly and cheerfully as he could: "My name is Gideon, Mr. Dane, George Gideon – Commander of the C.I.D. And I don't know about you, but I'm starving. How does the idea of coffee and sandwiches appeal?"

Dane stared at him, as if unable to believe his ears.

"I – I would like that very much," he said.

His voice, once he stopped whining, was quiet, cultured, almost pedantic in the way it gave each syllable precisely the correct stress. And Gideon noticed that behind the greasy, matted beard, and the layers of dirt on his neck, cheeks and forehead, there was a scholar's face, with a high forehead and deep-set, sensitive eyes. What in heaven's name, he wondered, could have happened to have turned such a man into such a mess? A disastrous love affair? Family problems? Professional frustration? Overwork? Not that it was his business to go into that. He was a policeman, not a psychiatrist, thank God.

He rapped on the door, and commanded one of the constables to bring the coffee and sandwiches. Then he motioned Dane towards one of the two plain wooden chairs — the only seating accommodation interrogation rooms ever seemed to afford — and lowered his own massive bulk into the other. Now that he and the drop-out were in close proximity, he became aware of a strong, almost overpowering smell of whisky. He wouldn't have been surprised to learn that sometime during the day, Dane had consumed half a bottle or more. And to his admittedly inexperienced nose, it smelt like high-quality stuff.

But how could Dane have obtained it — and where could he have consumed it, with the pubs, and every other conceivable drinking-place, having been under such massive surveillance all day?

Gideon's mind returned to the idea he had had earlier that day, the belief that Dane must have a friend, or, at any rate, a *befriender*: someone in the fashionable residential part of Wimbledon who took pity on him, and allowed him to slip into his home and doss down whenever he pleased.

The house-to-house search of that area had drawn a blank, certainly: but house-to-house searchers were human. They could slip up; they could be deceived and, in a hurried search over a wide area, were powerless if no one answered the door!

Dane, becoming restless at the long silence, shifted uneasily in his chair and suddenly gave way to a spasm of coughing. The smell of whisky was so strong now that Gideon felt that he only had to strike a match, for the whole room to go up in flames like a Christmas pudding.

Dane's "befriender", whoever he or she was, had certainly been generous with drink. The man must have been plied with, or given access to, whisky until he was almost senseless — didn't know what he was doing or saying . . .

Gideon sprang up from his chair, his own brain suddenly an inferno of speculation.

Dane, an acknowledged expert on explosives, could probably

138

become a mine of information on fire-raising when plied with a few drinks. Supposing someone had been *using* him, tapping his vast resources of technical knowledge, adopting an anagram of his name to try to frame him, perhaps even deliberately staging fires at factories in areas which Dane was frequenting?

That would explain a great deal.

Gideon wasn't sure that it didn't account for *everything*, except the powder found on Dane's coat, and he already had dark suspicions about that.

At that moment, the coffee and sandwiches arrived. Dane and Gideon both tackled them ravenously, Dane because he was literally starving, Gideon because he was suddenly in the greatest hurry of his life.

With iron self-discipline, he waited courteously until Dane had swallowed his last mouthful.

Then, softly but with the tension of a giant spring under a thousand tons of pressure, he said: "I'm going to ask you a few questions now, Dane. But don't worry. Not one of them will concern yourself. I am very much more anxious to know about – your friend, Dante."

*   *   *

Timothy Dane's eyes widened: the whites of them showed up against the dirt on his face almost as if he were doing an Al Jolson impersonation.

"My friend? Then you don't – you don't think *I'm* Dante?"

"No, I do not," Gideon told him. "I think – "

Speaking less gently now, and with a desperate urgency, he outlined his theory. Dane confirmed it at every point – except one.

"I *do* have a friend, he *does* live in Wimbledon, he *does* – as you call it – ply with me drinks, and it is perfectly correct that I have little recollection of what occurs when I go to see him." The pedantic voice contrasted so surrealistically with his appearance that he might have been an actor in make-up, especially since his manner was now no longer vague and rambling, but alert and concentrated. It was as though Dane was awake at last after going through a living nightmare; awake and thinking hard.

"But I am afraid it is simply not feasible that he could be Dante. He was interested in incendiary devices for purely professional reasons, because he is a high-ranking officer in the fire brigade."

"Is he, by God?" Gideon felt that electric shudder down his spine again; and remembered who he had been talking to when he had last felt it. "His name wouldn't be Cabot, by any chance?"

Dane shrugged.

"It's possible. I don't think he ever mentioned it."

"But the address? You must know that."

Dane spread out his hands helplessly.

"I am afraid things like street names and house numbers fly out of my head these days. I've been sensing my way around, like a cat. I could take you to the place blindfold, but —"

"Then take me to it," Gideon commanded. "Do you have a way of getting in?"

"Yes, a key, under a piece of crazy pav —"

"That's all we need, then," Gideon grunted. "Let's go, Dane, and pray that we're in time."

He glanced at his watch, and told himself there was a fat chance of that. It was already eleven forty-five.

He seized Dane by the arm, and virtually bundled him to the door. The constable outside opened it at his knock, and stared aghast, as Gideon rushed their star prisoner down the stairs, along a corridor, and out into the street.

At one point, a totally bewildered Farrant appeared, and actually attempted to bar Gideon's way.

"Do you need help, sir? Shall I arrange an escort —"

"You'll arrange bloody well nothing until you're asked to do so," Gideon roared. "But if you want to get busy, spread it around the station that the Dante emergency is still on. And so — unless we're a lot luckier than we deserve to be — is the Inferno ..."

Farrant blanched, and rushed off down the corridor. Gideon,

now almost dragging Dane behind him, charged out of the station and into the car park. A couple of seconds later, his Rover was tearing through the deserted streets of Wimbledon at very close to eighty miles an hour.

He pulled up near the alley where Dane had given Sergeant Baker the slip nearly twelve hours before.

"Think you can find your way from here?" he asked.

"Yes. This will do splendidly."

Once out of the car, their rôles were reversed, and Dane was amost dragging Gideon along the pavement, past rows of trim semi-detached suburban houses. Gideon recognised a street name: Palford Gardens. This was one of the roads where a house-to-house search had been held. But who would dream of searching the house of a fire-brigade chief?

"Here we are, Commander," Dane said, and halted outside No. 67.

A cold sense of fear swept over Gideon when he saw that the place was dark and empty. And the feeling became glacial when he glanced at his watch and saw that it was eleven fifty-three.

Dane stooped and found the doorkey without groping or stumbling, and a moment later, they were in No. 67's hall. Gideon clicked on the lights. The first thing that caught his eye was a framed certificate in the hall, announcing the presentation of a medal to Christopher James Cabot for exemplary bravery in rescuing the lives of . . .

No time for that now. Gideon snatched his eyes away, and began a lightning search of the house. First he went into the lounge, and saw the capacious drinks cabinet, significantly unlocked.

Dane walked over to it, and picked up a bottle of whisky.

Gideon was about to take it from him; but something made him hesitate.

Dane stood for a moment, staring down at the bottle. Then he said, with bitter self-reproach: "It certainly proved to be fire-water in my case, didn't it?"

Gideon could only guess what it was costing him to do it, but slowly he forced his fingers open and let the bottle fall.

It had hardly hit the carpet before Gideon was continuing his search of the ground floor, at the rate of a room a second.

A pale but determined-looking Dane caught up with him when he was giving the same treatment to the first floor, and was immediately behind him when he went up the short staircase to the loft, and discovered Cabot's laboratory.

It was a small room, its space almost completely filled by a crude trestle table. On its top were bottles of liquid, phials of powder, and eighty or ninety glass globes, about the size of cricket balls, arranged in rows as neatly as toy soldiers. Through the glass of each globe could be glimpsed a whitish-grey powder, perhaps the Dante incendiary substance that had been "found" on Dane's coat.

"What are these? Some sort of incendiary grenades?" asked Gideon.

Dane nodded. Suddenly, his face was almost the same shade as the powder, a deathly pallor supplying the white, the coating of dirt the grey.

"The most dangerous sort, I am afraid," he said. "One of these, lobbed over the wall at the right spot in the right kind of factory, would create an instant – "

"Inferno?" said Gideon.

There was a pause. Dane swayed, and almost fell. He clutched at a corner of the trestle table. The glass globes rattled against each other, and Gideon's heart turned over. Then Dane righted himself and stood back from the table.

"Inferno's the word," he said. His voice sank to an odd whisper, half the words being almost lost in his beard.

"If – if four or five factories in the same area are hit s-simultaneously, it could equal the – the Dresden fire storm."

Gideon glanced back at the table and was suddenly as close to blind panic as he had ever been in his life.

There were significant gaps in those trim rows of globes, indicating that Cabot had picked up several to stuff into his pockets, or a suitcase, before leaving.

Several?

Gideon counted the gaps in the rows, and made the total more

142

than thirty.

If four or five blazing factories could create a fire storm, what would thirty do?

The answer was – literally – unthinkable.

Gideon's brain reeled back from it: refused to accept that the situation was real, the risk genuine.

But the facts spoke for themselves, giving the nightmare that had been haunting him all day a terrifying shape, solidity, reality.

The unthinkable had to be thought, the unimaginable imagined, the unfaceable faced.

Cabot *had* the means at his disposal to start a Great Fire of London.

He had them with him in a car, of unknown make, year and number; and had, at an unspecified time within the past hour, left Wimbledon to go . . . where?

North towards Fulham, Gideon's own home town, with plenty of light industries, including paint and chemical factories galore? North-East towards Clapham and Battersea, still one of the big power centres of London? Or South towards Merton, Morden and the new, booming industrial estates round Mitcham and Purley?

There was no knowing.

The first flare-up, then, could come at any second, anywhere over a twenty-mile area – an area which would be wide open to a man who knew what he was doing, throwing carefully-aimed fire bombs from a speeding car.

The special police patrols, which had been on guard at key factories until two hours before, had been sent home on Gideon's own advice, phoned to the head of Uniform just after the fire-brigade meeting.

The fire brigade itself, of course, would be standing down on the stroke of midnight, in seven minutes' time, and even though a special appeal broadcast or phoned to all stations *might* persuade a few faithfuls to stay on duty, the vast majority of firemen would suspect a hoax – Gideon getting on their backs again – and insist on contacting their Union for an okay.

There were the Green Goddess units, of course, to be

alerted –

Christ! What was he thinking of? There was Scott-Marle, the Home Secretary, perhaps even the Prime Minister to be alerted!

With his thoughts still in tumult, but with the need for action over-riding everything, Gideon half-charged, half-crashed downstairs to the hall, and picked up the phone.

He began by ringing Scott-Marle's home number: a thing he had done only a handful of times before.

Sir Reginald rose to the occasion with a calm decisiveness which made Gideon's respect for him soar.

"I entirely agree, George, that the Home Office must be brought in on this right away, and so should our Anti-Terrorist branch. I'll also get on to the B.B.C. and I.B.A. to put out special announcements. There's a risk that that may start a panic, but – "

"It'll be all to the good," said Gideon grimly, "if it panics the strikers."

"And as soon as we get the details of Cabot's car – the computer in Traffic Records should give them to us fast enough – I'll see that every Panda and area car is on the streets hunting for it." Scott-Marle's voice was suddenly less decisive and more anxious: the horror of the situation had obviously taken a moment to sink in. "If only we had an hour to act in, instead of minutes – "

Gideon nearly said, "If only we had minutes, instead of seconds," but there was no point in heightening the tension. It was almost unbearable already. Instead:

"I'll get on to Wimbledon police station myself, sir," he said. "They're nearest to the scene, and have already been alerted. If they can send squad cars and motor cyclists down all the main roads radiating out from Wimbledon, there's just a chance – "

He broke off, aware that he was clutching at straws.

What sort of chance was there that they could catch up with a fire-brigade chief who knew the area better than they did, and who had up to an *hour's* start on them?

There was a click as Scott-Marle, too hard-pressed for courtesies, went off the line. It sounded like a click of contempt.

Frustration built up inside Gideon until his heart was racing as fast as those flying seconds.

There *had* to be something he could do, other than sit and wait for the first flash to light up the sky – a flash that within minutes could become a storm, sucking the air away from the lungs of anyone who tried to fight it.

Factory . . . Factory . . . Somewhere early in the case he had heard Farrant mention a factory – Mortimer's Paints of Morden. Of course. Dane had been originally spotted by the police hanging about its entrance.

Gideon's heart was now beating so fast that he could hardly breathe. It was as if a fire storm was already robbing his lungs of air.

In the past, he remembered, the Dante fires had always "followed Dane about". Cabot, in other words, had always chosen factories in which he knew his "friend" was taking an interest. It was therefore probable that he had been devising a blaze at Mortimer's before Dane's arrest had altered his plans. Probably he had already got Dane to tell him its most vulnerable spots.

What place in the world, then, was he more likely to choose for tonight's first inferno?

Gideon shouted out to Dane, and the drop-out came hurrying down the stairs. He had a bathroom towel in his hand, and looked as though he had actually been washing his face. Most of the dirt was gone; but the skin still looked white-grey.

"We're going to an old haunt of yours," Gideon told him. "Mortimer's Paints at Morden. Do you think you can show me the way?"

"With no trouble at all, Commander."

Thirty seconds later, they had locked up and left the house. Three minutes later, they had found, and were climbing into Gideon's Rover, parked some streets away. A church clock somewhere nearby chimed midnight, a reminder that at that very moment, every fire station, large or small, was being locked up and left, too.

The freshening wind was whistling round the car as Gideon

started up the engine. It seemed to be roaring past at hurricane force as the Rover sped out of Wimbledon down the Merton-Morden road at more than eighty miles per hour.

There were few cars, and hardly any people about. Everything looked so deserted that it was almost as though London itself had been locked up and left.

To the tender mercies of Dante.

17 Loot

At that moment, on the forecourt of the Haig garage at Aldgate, Matt Honiwell leant against the bonnet of a second-hand car (a 1968 Ford Capri, on offer at £385) and announced: "Right, lads, that's it. One last look round, and I'm calling it a night."

His men – Detective Sergeant Davis and Detective Constables Foster and Drake – tried hard not to sound relieved. Under Matt's direction, they had been searching the garage, and the Haig's flat above it, for the better part of four hours. They had worked frenziedly, with implacable determination, because Matt had told them they were avenging old Dick Meadows, one of the most popular men in the C.I.D.

Only Davis, an incurably argumentative little Welshman, had queried this.

"I 'eard Dick had taken a bashing from a lot of bloody rioters. We aren't going to catch rioters, are we, by hunting around petrol pumps at dead of night for God knows what?"

Patiently, Matt had explained Gideon's theory that the Blackfriars gang had deliberately engineered the attack on Meadows, to stop him watching the garage.

"And one thing's not a theory, but a *fact*," he had added. "The Blackfriars gang wants to keep the police away from this place, at all costs. I've had a telephone threat which testifies to that. And Commander Gideon's right: in the light of that threat, it does seem fishy that the first policeman who starts watching this place gets it in the neck."

Davis nodded, and seemed to agree. But it was simply not in the little Welshman to stop arguing for long.

"Perhaps it was just the Haig family they didn't want spied on. Perhaps we're just wasting our time here poking around after they've gone."

Matt had sighed.

"When you've been in the force as long as I have, Davis my lad, you'll realise that ninety-eight per cent of what we do turns out, in the end, to have been wasting time! But that doesn't usually apply to people following a Gideon hunch, which is what we're doing tonight. So stop arguing, and let's get on!"

It had sounded quite an inspiring speech at around a quarter past eight. It had still seemed impressive, when he had repeated it in different words at around nine and ten.

But when two more hours had gone by, with nothing remotely significant or incriminating to the Blackfriars gang turning up, even Matt had found it impossible to talk enthusiastically about Gideon's hunches.

He had not enjoyed breaking into the Haigs' flat, even though the search warrant gave him authority to do so. Rita Haig had suffered enough and, after all, it was to her intervention that Meadows owed his life. One consolation was that they couldn't mess the place up any more. All the rooms were in wild confusion, evidence of the tremendous haste with which the Haigs had packed up and left. But beneath the confusion was abundant evidence of comfortable living. The sons each had expensive hi-fi "music centres" in the bedrooms; their colour T.V. was one of the costliest models on the market; the kitchen contained every modern gadget from a luxury freezer to the latest dishwashing machine, and Rita's bedroom wardrobe had three fur coats worth several hundred pounds apiece. It seemed unlikely that a garage would have produced enough to pay for all this; the shady activities which Lenny had been mixed up with all over the East End had obviously been highly lucrative. But it was hard to see why the Blackfriars mob should have objected to the police keeping a watch on a few luxury goods, and nothing else had come to light at all, even though floorboards had been lifted up in search of hidden stores of guns, the drawers removed from desks and dressing-tables and carefully tapped in search of hidden compartments, and even the tank in the airing cupboard dismantled and inspected in case it contained drugs or diamonds.

The garage had been subjected to the same treatment, and that included the equipment in the forecourt, from the petrol pumps to the pump attendant's till. The used cars on offer were not forgotten either: seats were lifted, boots opened, bonnets raised, even glove compartments explored. But here, once again, hours of work had resulted only in bemusement and growing memories.

Matt's men were getting cold too. The wind was whistling round the forecourt, growing fiercer and more bitter every minute; and worse, it was causing an infuriating creaking and clanging to come from the large metallic globe, advertising GLOBALPOWER petrol, on the garage roof.

"One last look round," Matt said again; but he made it one last look *up*, shining his torch for the hundredth time on that ten-foot-wide advertising monstrosity. The globe glinted faintly in the torchlight, almost as if it was shining with its own radiance, and had just touched down on that roof from outer space.

"Perhaps *that's* the object we're not intended to observe," Detective Sergeant Davis suggested heavily. "Full it is, maybe, with little green men who don't like us to watch them doing tap-dancing practice on that roof."

A gust of wind struck the globe with full force at that moment. It seemed to emit a creaking groan, and toppled halfway off its base. It looked as if at any moment it would come crashing down on the forecourt.

"I'd duck if I were you, Taffy," grinned Matt. "I don't think your little green men appreciate Welsh humour."

Davis did not grin back. In the reflected torchlight, his face was suddenly thoughtful in the extreme.

"Do you suppose there's any chance of us getting up there and looking inside that thing?"

149

"I've been wondering just that all night," said Matt. "But the only way up is through a skylight in one of the flat's bedrooms, and once you're up, you're on a very exposed stretch of roof, with a sheer twenty-foot drop on either side. And if that bloody ball took it into its head to break loose at that moment . . ." He shrugged and shuddered. "There've been enough tragedies in this case," he added softly. "I'm not going to risk any more."

The globe, though, seemed to be almost mesmerising him. He could not take his eyes off it. Or his torch. Or his mind . . .

Supposing Lenny had been given something by the Blackfriars gang to keep safe for them? He might well have thought of hiding it in that globe. It was only a few steps – upwards! – from his bedroom, and on a quiet night, wouldn't be difficult or dangerous to reach. It was probably hollow, and almost certainly had an inspection flap somewhere, through which almost any objects could be inserted.

That would explain at a stroke why the Blackfriars mob had been so insistent that the garage should not be kept under surveillance. They wouldn't have been able to touch that globe without a watcher seeing every move.

Last night, there hadn't been any watcher but they would still have been stymied, this time by the eighty-mile per hour gales.

Then, today, when the gales died down and they were ready to act, they'd spotted Dick Meadows over the street observing them and had taken violent action against him.

What had happened then?

Had the mob moved in and emptied the globe, or had they been too rattled, finding that they had nearly killed a cop?

The Haigs had taken fright, and bolted from the scene. Was it possible that the Blackfriars mob had done the same?

In that case, they'd be out there, somewhere, watching and waiting for him and his men to leave, so that at last they could tackle that globe.

They weren't standing as close to it as he was, probably didn't realise that it was on the point of –

"Bloody hell, sir – look OUT!"

It was a frantic shout from Davis, reinforced by similar yells from the constables.

Some tortured rivet at the base of the globe had given way, and the whole nightmare structure was suddenly toppling, rolling, falling —

Davis and the constables took to their heels, and were off the forecourt in two great leaps apiece.

Matt, lost in excitement at his theory, reacted far more slowly. He had taken less than half a leap when the great metal ball came crashing down on to the concrete.

It landed barely a foot behind him, shaking the concrete beneath him with earthquake force.

A jarring sensation shot up his legs, as though he'd just taken a six-foot jump. He staggered for a second; then a muscle gave in his right ankle, and he tripped and fell headlong.

The shock momentarily blinded him to everything. It deafened him, too, to the almost hysterical shouts of Davis, Foster and Drake, who were screaming at him that the ball *had started to roll his way.*

*   *   *

It didn't, in fact, roll far for the simple reason that almost instantaneously it started to split asunder.

Basically, it was evidently constructed in two halves, like a monster Easter egg; and the split occurred near the ground, at the base of the central join. Here the bottoms of the two halves parted company, creating a triangular aperture, about two foot high at its apex, which looked uncannily like the door of a spaceship sliding open.

No little green men came out. But something equally green, and equally startling did.

As Matt rolled over, and peered up at the monstrous mass of metal that had so nearly crushed him, he was aware of an odd rustling all round him. Then something hit him full in the mouth — something paper-thin and crinkly, but driven with such force by a gust of wind that it stung like a whiplash.

He groped for his torch, turned it full on to the globe, and grinned as he realised what had hit him.

Bank notes – pound notes, fivers, tenners – were flying out of the triangle like wasps streaming out of a nest.

No wonder the Blackfriars mob had been so desperate to stop the garage being watched. In that crazy globe towering above it had been hidden all the proceeds of their murderous £300,000 snatch.

18 The Waiting Game

Matt began to struggle to his feet. But then, quite deliberately, he fell back on the ground, realistically writhing and groaning.

Davis came rushing up, the two constables close behind him, and dropped down on one knee beside Matt.

"What happened, sir? Did it get your foot — "

He broke off, gasping and clawing bank-notes from his face.

Before he could find his voice, Matt whispered:

"Ignore them. Pretend you haven't seen them. All you're concerned about is getting me to the car. I've lost an arm and a leg and am bleeding horribly."

"You've lost a — "

Davis might be whimsically Welsh; but he had a shrewd brain, and used it. After a second's floundering, he caught on to Honiwell's plan.

With the help of the two constables, neither of whom seemed to have noticed the notes flying past them in the darkness, Davis lifted Matt bodily and carried him gently across the forecourt to where the police car was parked.

He was stretched out on the back seat, with Davis sitting beside him. The two constables sat in front, with Foster taking the wheel.

Under Matt's direction, Foster backed the Panda out of the forecourt, and turned right down the street which the garage faced. It was a street of struggling small businesses: shabby cafés, betting shops, newsagents with windows full of girlie magazines and a couple of odorous takeaways. Everything was closed now. Except for the street lamps, not a light showed anywhere. The silence was so complete that it was somehow menacing. None of the men in the car could forget that this was a police-hating area. Over the shops were dozens of windows, blankly mirroring the orange street lamps. Behind any of those windows there could be watching eyes.

Davis glanced up at them uneasily.

"I take it, sir, that all this is for the benefit of anyone spying on us, right?"

"Absolutely right, Taffy," said Matt. "And you can be bloody sure we *are* being watched, too. You realise what was in that globe?"

Davis had worked out the answer to that one, long before.

"£300,000, approximately, I'd say, sir, and with the way the wind's blowing it about, 'approximately' is the word!"

The two constables in the front seat gasped. Foster, behind the wheel, turned his head. He was a small man, small as a constable could be; and his eyes were wide as a scared rabbit's.

"The whole of the loot from the Blackfriars snatch?"

"That's right, Foster, you're coming on," said Matt.

"But, forgive me, sir, but I still don't get why you pretended to be injured."

"Then put yourself in the Blackfriars mob's place. For forty-eight hours, they've been desperate to get their hands on that loot, but have been frustrated again and again. Their final attempt involved staging a riot to get rid of Meadows, but they overdid it and nearly killed him. The Haigs bolted from the scene, and my guess is the Blackfriars mob did the same, until things cooled down. Probably they planned to come back once it was dark, provided that everything seemed quiet. But everything hasn't been quiet for them, has it? We've been here poking around for four solid hours. They must have been watching us in a cold sweat, terrified that at any moment we'd start searching the globe. And they must have nearly had heart failure when, just as we were leaving, they saw the globe fall flat on top of me.

"But what happened then, from their point of view? They

154

probably heard the three of you yelling at me to watch out. Then they saw you all carrying me into the car. They are bound to think that their luck's changed at last. The hated Haig-killer Honiwell has got his come-uppance, and been carted off to hospital with a crushed leg. All the fuzz have gone, leaving the coast absolutely clear. And the loot is no longer high up and inaccessible. It's there waiting for them on that forecourt like a ripe plum that's just fallen from a tree. They're not going to resist that, are they? I can almost guarantee you that as soon as their spy can get to a phone, the Blackfriars mob will be there in that forecourt scooping up their takings."

Davis chuckled and rubbed his hands.

"So we double-back and catch 'em as red-handed as any gang has ever been!"

"That's the idea, boyo," Matt grinned. He sat up and started to give detailed instructions to Foster. "Right here. Then left by the traffic lights. Then right again ... Watch out for a back street called Blackwater Way. I think it'll bring us out right behind the Haig garage. Oh, and Drake. Contact the station, will you? We could do with all the reinforcements we can get. Don't forget, this is the mob that shot a girl bank clerk just for sneezing."

A sudden awed silence fell on the car. They were all armed. Matt had drawn revolvers and cartridges and doled them out before they'd left the Yard. But no one, except Matt himself, had ever been involved in a shoot-out before.

Honiwell did a quick calculation. There were six cars on all-night patrol in the area, all in direct contact with Aldgate Pump police station. With luck, there would be plenty of time for a couple of those cars to be called back to the station, supplied with guns, and then sent round to join them in Blackwater Way. That would mean three carloads of armed policemen versus a mob of five. Not bad odds. Perhaps enough to persuade even the trigger-happy Blackfriars hoods to come quietly.

There was a crackling whine as Drake switched on the police radio. Then everyone in the car tensed, instantly sensing that something strange was going on. Instead of the usual procession

155

of radio messages – "Car A6, proceed at once to Kilburn High Road", and so on – what sounded like an emergency announcement was being made.

"All area cars, pandas on patrol duty and operational vehicles on standby north of the Thames must proceed south. All area cars, pandas on patrol duty and operational vehicles on standby south of the Thames must proceed at once to the Wimbledon area. All drivers must keep in touch, and await further instructions. The arsonist known as Dante is believed to be at large in the area, and to be planning an immediate attack on paint and chemical factories, using incendiary grenades. Christopher James Cabot, fire-brigade officer of 67, Palford Gardens, Wimbledon, is urgently wanted for questioning in connection with the case. Height: 6ft 4ins. Hair: grey. Probably wearing fire-brigade uniform, and driving a small red 1975 Citröen, registration no. UHL 4569 N." There was a pause, then the voice began again. "This is an emergency. This is an emergency. All area cars, pandas on patrol duty and operational vehicles on standby north of the Thames must proceed . . ."

"That's enough," Matt said, and Drake switched the radio off.

Another silence fell – this time, not so much an awed as a stunned one.

"Wonder if the fire-brigade strike's still on," said Matt at length. "If it is, and Dante's really on the loose, then, Christ, this *is* an emergency."

"Are we going to go south of the Thames?" asked Foster.

"Not us," said Matt. "We aren't on patrol or standby, but on special duty." His voice became low and grim. "And I'm afraid it's going to be *very* special duty. We've no choice but to take on the Blackfriars mob on our own."

He glanced round him, at Davis, enthusiastic and excited; Drake, quiet and dubious, and Foster, looking more like a scared rabbit than ever. And being Matt Honiwell, he thought too of Davis' pretty wife Wendy and their two children, aged two and three; of Drake's girl friend, a formidable-looking policewoman called Barbara; and of Foster's young wife Melanie, a blue-eyed blonde in hospital at the moment following

156

a miscarriage. For all their sakes, he hoped that it wouldn't come to a shoot-out, yet in his heart of hearts, he couldn't see the situation developing any other way.

"Ah, well," Davis was saying, his Welshness more evident than ever. "We're four men against three men and two women and if they're trigger-happy, we'll just have to teach them to be bloody trigger-miserable."

Drake and Foster laughed, Foster so nervously that he might have been hiccuping.

Matt tried to grin, but failed.

The car was coming to the end of Blackwater Way. On their left, behind two hoardings advertising Globalpower Petrol, was the back of the Haig garage.

"Pull in here," Matt commanded.

The car halted at a point exactly opposite a gap between the hoardings. From here, they had a clear view of the forecourt, and could even see the top of the fallen globe. To the right of the hoardings was a concrete path leading past the garage on to the forecourt itself: a back way in which might prove useful for sneaking up on the gang, Matt thought. Although they'd have to get out of the car to use it — it was less than two foot across.

"All we have to do now is wait," said Matt.

"For death or glory, boyos," said Taffy Davis cheerfully, and could not understand why no one laughed at all.

*　　*　　*

"How much f—— longer are we going to have to wait?" demanded Sid Stannet, and even here, in the heart of his luxury hideout, surrounded by half-a-dozen armed henchmen, the king of the London racketeers was visibly shaking and sweating.

He was a plump, pink-complexioned man in his early forties, with a bald head that looked so shiny that it seemed as if at any moment it would make the old joke come true, and start to steam. His eyes — normally black and piercing, but tonight looking bloodshot and bleary — turned on Alec Hobbs and the two A10 men with a ferocious glare.

"There's no law that says I have to go along with this bloody

157

stupid game of yours," he said. "This maniac cop is after my blood. Why can't you simply arrest him as soon as he shows his face? What's the *point* of you all hiding and listening to what he has to say to me?" Suddenly his face turned crimson with anger – an anger that was near to hysteria. "It's a trap of some sort, isn't it? Admit it. It's a f------ trap."

Alec Hobbs sighed deeply, and attempted, for at least the twentieth time in the past three hours, to calm the racketeer down.

"Sid, Sid, *Sid*," he said reproachfully. "Do I really have to explain the whole thing again? Riddell is in no position to trap you or anybody else. He's deep in trouble himself, subject to suspension and a full police inquiry."

Stannet brightened and laughed thickly. He had been drinking double whiskies all evening, and they were beginning to slur his speech.

"That'll teach him to tangle with Sid Stannet! That'll teach all of you to try and – to try and get the better of me."

Alec refused to get ruffled.

"Quite right, Sid, we all admit you've been too clever for us," he said casually. "And you've certainly written 'FINIS' to the career of poor old Tom Riddell. When he comes here tonight, you'll find he's a pathetic wreck of a man. All we want you to do is just listen to him talking for a few minutes, so that we can assess what sort of a state he's in. It is something that will greatly help our internal police inquiries, as Mr. Stephenson and Mr. Rance here will testify."

Stephenson and Rance both grunted their agreement. It was beyond them to do more. Stephenson, with his official Uniform mind, was still of the opinion that all this was preposterously irregular. Jimmy Rance, convinced that Tom really was half out of his mind, could not see what good eavesdropping and spying on him would do. What was more, it was getting so late now that he was beginning to have grave doubts if Riddell would turn up at all.

Only Hobbs still believed that Gideon had known what he was doing when he had suggested this exercise. George's words rang through his mind now. "Yes, I *am* asking for trouble . . . for Sid Stannet. He's known to be a hysterical type. There's just a chance that Riddell will succeed in breaking his nerve. And I'd rather *that* happened than that he was left grinning all over his face."

Well, one of Gideon's predictions had come true, at least, Alec told himself. Stannet was definitely *not* grinning all over his face.

At the moment, he was pacing the room, a long, flashy lounge the size of a small ballroom, with a grand piano at one end, complete with a Liberace-style candelabra. When he neared the piano, his heavy tread made the candelabra rattle. He started as violently as if he had heard an explosion.

Then he swung round on Alec, glowering more fiercely than ever.

"One thing's agreed, I hope. I'm not letting that mad cop loose on me with a gun. The boys will frisk and disarm him before he takes a step past the front door. Okay?"

"Okay," said Alec.

"And – and this talk with me isn't going to become an all-night grilling, or anything like it. A few minutes. That's what you said, wasn't it?"

Alec smiled, and his voice became more soothing than ever.

"That's what we said, Sid. That's what it'll be."

"All – all right then." Stannet was back at the drinks cabinet now, pouring himself yet another neat double. "But – but I warn you: it's all off if your man doesn't show soon. Say by twelve thirty at the latest – "

One of Stannet's henchmen came in, a burly tough who looked as if he'd started life as a chucker-out, but who was now struggling to give the place class by posing as a butler.

"A Mr. Riddell to see you, Sid."

Stannet started twice as violently as when the candelabra had rattled.

"Have you searched him?"

"Of course, Sid. He had one revolver, loaded. Nothing else."

"Right, then." Stannet swallowed hard, and glaring round at

159

Hobbs, Stephenson and Rance, waved them towards some plush scarlet floor-to-ceiling curtains that concealed a bay window. "Don't let's keep the gentleman hanging around, Bruiser. Show him in."

He looked almost relieved that the waiting game was over, until he saw the expression on Riddell's face, as the Yard man came striding into the room.

*　　*　　*

For George Gideon, the waiting game was just beginning.

Two minutes before, he had brought the Rover to a halt outside the entrance to the Mortimer Paint factory at Morden. It was the first time the speedometer needle had dropped below eighty since they had left Wimbledon: he shuddered to think how many traffic regulations he had broken.

Everything, everywhere still seemed uncannily deserted. He had hardly sighted a car anywhere on the route. The road ahead and behind still seemed totally clear. The gaunt outline of the paint factory itself reared on his left, dark and empty-looking and still, apart from an occasional creaking and clanging, which was probably the wind knocking over piled-up cans, or causing metal doors to shake and rattle.

Only one thing testified to the fact that London was not a giant, deserted lock-up tonight. The police radio, which Gideon had had installed in his Rover, was repeating over and over again Scott-Marle's special emergency instructions. *"All area cars, pandas on patrol duty, and operational vehicles on standby must proceed . . ."* Gideon tried to calculate how many police cars must now be pouring into the Wimbledon vicinity. He reckoned between eighty and a hundred. If only Cabot held off his attack for a quarter of an hour longer, that number of cars would provide saturation coverage of the South London industrial estates. And after that, the moment he showed up in any of them, he'd have a police car on his tail before he'd covered another hundred yards.

There was one big snag to all this, though. Nothing was more unlikely than that Cabot *would* hold off his attack. And if he struck *now* what could eighty, a hundred, or even a million police cars do in the face of a massive blaze, an air-sucking firestorm, an inferno?

Gideon turned hot, then cold all over. The wind whistling past the Rover – a south-easterly gale, as far as he could reckon – made him think of how easily a blaze like that could spread towards the centre of the Metropolis. He had a terrifying vision of all London – St. Paul's Cathedral, Westminister Abbey, Oxford Street stores, great office tower blocks and humble East End tenements alike – exploding into sheets of flame; of Big Ben crashing downwards like a giant redwood in a forest fire.

The radio interrupted his nightmare reverie.

"... possibly wearing fire-brigade uniform, and driving a small red 1975 Citroën, registration number VHL 4569 N ..."

Good, he thought. The Yard computer room hadn't wasted much time in coming up with the details of Cabot's car. And with the road as clear as it was tonight, it should be possible to spot it from quite a distance.

But there was an awkward corollary to that. Cabot would be able to spot *him* from quite a distance, too. And if he saw a large Rover waiting for him outside the very factory gates, he'd turn off and launch his attack elsewhere.

Launch his attack –

Gideon found himself staring at the entrance gates of Mortimer Paints. They were typical factory gates, made of wire mesh, about seven foot high, with a fence of similar height and wire-mesh construction stretching away on either side. Beyond, as far as he could see in the darkness, was just a concrete yard, with no building near except a low, single-storey structure that looked as if it housed offices.

It suddenly struck him that nothing spectacularly inflammable would happen, even if the most powerful incendiary grenade in the world was chucked from a car travelling past here.

Baffled, he turned to Dane. The drop-out was sitting beside him, hunched and still, staring at the distant factory outline as if mesmerised.

161

"Penny for 'em," said Gideon heavily.

"I – er – I beg your pardon, Commander?"

"You're brooding about this factory, aren't you? I'd like to share your thoughts."

Dane frowned.

"I seem – seem to remember Cabot asking me things about this place. I was trying to remember what I'd told him. But it's all so hopelessly vague and hazy."

"I can tell you Question No. 1 that Cabot would have asked you," Gideon said. "And that's where an incendiary bomb would cause the most spectacular – "

Dane started so violently that the top of his head only just missed banging against the roof.

"Ah," said Gideon, tensely. "Coming back to you now, is it?"

"Yes. Very definitely."

"And you told him – what?"

Dane rubbed his recently-washed cheeks, as if their unfamiliar cleanness bothered him.

"I – I think I mentioned a road I'd explored at the side of the factory, leading close to a tank complex. 'There's your real fire risk,' I said. 'It would only take a match dropped there to – ' "

Gideon had already started the car.

"Which way is this road? Behind us or ahead?"

"I think it's back about fifty yards – "

Gideon abruptly reversed. His palms were so sticky with sweat that it took him a second to get a grip on the clutch.

The end of the factory grounds swung into view. The wire-mesh fence turned off at right angles to the road, and alongside it ran what looked like a mud track, separating the fence from a patch of grass and gorse.

"This it?"

"I – can't say for sure, Commander, but I believe so."

"Then I'll be a believer too," said Gideon decisively.

He swung the Rover off the road, thankful for its healthy springs as he bumped it recklessly over the kerb, and on to the grassy track.

162

"How long before we come to this — what d'you call it — tank complex?"

"Two hundred yards or so, if I remember correctly."

Dane evidently did "remember correctly". After almost exactly two hundred yards, they came to a point where the main factory was only fifty feet or so beyond the fence; and adjoining the building were several long, low tanks, the nearest of them barely twenty-five feet from the wall.

Gideon stopped the car and wound down the window, to see as much as possible through the dark. There were two large signs beside the tanks. He could make out the letters "NO S" on one and "INFL" on the other. He guessed that they said "NO SMOKING" and "HIGHLY INFLAMMABLE" respectively.

"One spark anywhere near those tanks," Dane murmured, "and flaming spirit will spread everywhere."

Gideon was still peering through the dark.

"Easy lobbing distance," he noted. "But not so easy for someone throwing at car-window level. The grenade would have to clear a seven-foot fence, and then travel over twenty-five feet."

"What's to stop Cabot getting out of his car?"

"Nothing," said Gideon very softly and tensely. "In fact, if he comes here, that's just what he is bound to do."

Sudden hope was beginning to flame in his brain; a hope that the Dante horror could be halted before it began.

He started up the Rover, and swung it left off the track, into the heart of the patch of scrubland. After a couple of hundred yards, they came to a tangle of stinging nettles and brambles tall enough to hide a good part of the car from anyone driving along the track.

Not ideal, thought Gideon, but it would have to do. He eased the Rover behind the tangle, then sprang out and, with Dane close behind him, raced back to the track. As he ran, he was making furious calculations.

Cabot would have to drive down the track to about this point, and then, if he had any sense, he would turn the Citroën back to face the road. You need to think in terms of split-second

163

getaways when you're making a sea of flaming spirit just the other side of a fence.

Having turned the car, Cabot would get out, armed with two or possibly three of his deadly glass grenades, and begin to lob them, one by one, over the fence in the direction of the tanks.

"Do these globes go off instantly?" Gideon asked.

Dane shook his head.

"Not quite. There's a liquid core that has to be exposed to the air for a second or so. Then it takes another second to ignite the powder. The explosion wouldn't happen until two or three seconds after the globe hit its target."

Enough time for Cabot to chuck at least a couple of them, Gideon thought, and then leap back to the car and get safely away.

But if he could be taken by surprise from behind a split second before he lobbed the first grenade, or better still, the moment he left the car –

Gideon needed no telling how dangerous the operation would be. He had no gun on him – no weapon of any sort, not even a penknife. And he would be struggling to arrest a man armed with devices as dangerous as Mills bombs with their pins taken out. If one of those globes was thrown at him, or was dropped on the ground, or even cracked, then he, Cabot, Dane, the car – all would be engulfed in a private inferno from which there would be no hope whatever of escaping alive. But, thought Gideon grimly, if creating a private inferno was the only way of saving all London from a public one –

Suddenly there was no time for *ifs*, only for action.

"Quick!" breathed Gideon, and grasping Dane's arm, pulled him down behind the largest patch of scrub in sight.

He thought he had heard the sound of a car, and now he could see the outline of one, bumping along the dirt track towards him.

It had no lights, and a gust of wind was blowing dust in his eyes, so that he could barely see, but it sounded very much like a small Citroën.

19 Blood Money

At exactly that moment, thirteen miles to the north across London, a white Ford Estate car drew up outside the Haig garage in Aldgate. Both nearside doors opened. Five people got out. It was hard to be sure from his long-distance vantage point behind the posters in Blackwater Way, but it looked to Matt Honiwell as if there were three men and two women, which, Lenny Haig had told him, was the composition of the Blackfriars Street gang.

"Right. Everybody out," Matt breathed. "And I don't mean on strike!"

A second or two later, he was out of the police car, and walking down the two-foot-wide concrete path that formed the back way into the forecourt. Detective Sergeant Davis was hard behind him, his revolver already in his hand. The two constables, Drake and Foster, were rather hesitantly bringing up the rear.

Ahead of them, the five people from the estate car were now crossing the forecourt towards the fallen globe, and the £300,000 loot. At one point, they passed close to the one light that had been left burning in the forecourt: a bulb in a mock iron lantern hanging above the stairs that led up to the Haigs' flat.

Matt recognised Rita Haig — there was no mistaking her dark, flashing eyes — and four of her children: the three eighteen to twenty-year-old boys, Dick, John and Stephen, and the seventeen-year-old June.

Matt relaxed, and called over his shoulder:

"It's all right, lads. It's only the Haig family. Obviously they've got over their fright, and come home."

"Then why are they making a beeline for that globe instead of heading for that flat? Ruddy suspicious, I call it," Taffy Davis breathed.

"I suppose they want to see what in the world's happened," Matt answered with a grin. "We'd better get them off the forecourt quickly, before the real Blackfriars mob shows up."

He broke into a quick stride, almost a run, and went towards the Haigs, shouting and waving. But the wind, now nearly back to gale force, was whipping across the forecourt straight into his face, snatching the words from his mouth and carrying them behind him. The Haigs did not hear either his shouts or his footsteps, a fact which very probably saved his life.

When he was less than ten yards away from them, the wind started carrying *their* remarks to *him*.

"Quick!" one of the Haig boys was saying to his mother. "We've only just got time to stash this lot. The cops might be here any minute."

And Rita replied: "Nah they won't, Stevie, not on your ruddy life. They'll be too bleeding scared arter what we did to their f-----g spy this afternoon . . ."

Matt, dazed – but not too dazed to think quickly – turned left and dived out of sight behind the globe.

A lot of things were suddenly clear to him, and became clearer every second as he heard the Haigs scooping up their loot.

He'd been hoodwinked all along the line, blinded by his sentimental sympathy for a family he'd made fatherless.

Now the facts were staring him in the face.

There wasn't merely a mysterious connection between the Haigs and the Blackfriars snatch gang.

The Haigs and the gang were one.

Rita was the leader. Her four eldest children were the members. And Lenny Haig had been asked – or told, depending on how henpecked a husband he'd been – to act as their driver.

He had probably agreed willingly enough. He had always lived on the edge of law-breaking. Having his family go into the hold-up business *en masse* may have amused him; perhaps it had even excited his imagination. But one thing was certain. When Lenny had heard those shots and screams coming from the raided bank, he had been sickened and appalled. That explained why an old "pro" like him had been careless enough to leave a thumbprint on the driving wheel. He had been reduced to a near-hysteria of shame and horror, far beyond remembering details like that.

A near-hysteria of shame and horror . . . Yes.

Matt had a sudden vision of Lenny, staring at a knothole in the wooden table of the Aldgate Pump interrogation room, his voice strained and hoarse as he'd answered questions about the gang. "There were five of them, I can tell you that. Two of 'em women, the rest men . . . Or – or boys. The women had the revolvers, the men sawn-off shotguns . . .Bloody murdering *gits*, the lot of them . . ."

The words had a terrible poignancy now Matt realised that Lenny had been talking about, passing judgment on, his own family. No wonder the tension inside the little garage owner had risen to lethal dimensions, particularly when he had been on the brink of naming Rita as the head of the gang.

"Leader? Oh. Oh, yeah. I sussed that out – no bother. It was . . .·it was . . ."

He had got no further, because, quite literally, he hadn't had the heart to. He had died with the secret on his lips – killed, almost certainly, by the shock of realising what sort of woman Rita really was; and what monsters she had turned his own kids into.

What had happened after that was easy to figure out. After Lenny's arrest, the Haigs had hidden their loot in the safest place they could think of, for fear of more calls from the police. In frantic haste, they must have crammed the notes through an inspection slit in the huge advertising globe. That explained why the notes were loose, not stacked in piles, as they must have been when they left the bank. The globe had been a perfect hiding place, except for one snag. The money couldn't be retrieved

167

from there as long as anyone was watching the garage.

That was why Rita had tricked him, Matt, into giving her that cheque, so that he could be blackmailed into giving the garage a wide berth, at least for one night.

The Haigs had no doubt intended to empty the globe during that night, and to have disappeared without trace by the morning. Their scheme had been ruined, first, by the eighty-mile-per-hour gale, which had made it totally impossible to get near the globe, let alone bring down £300,000 from it, during the night; and second, by the fact that he, Matt, had beaten the blackmail threat and had put Meadows on to watch the gang by the morning.

Rita had therefore staged that anti-police demonstration. She couldn't have found it difficult to do. She must have had a procession of East End friends coming to offer their sympathies over Lenny. Probably she'd pointed Meadows out to each of them, and said: "See? Even now, the fuzz can't let a poor widow be . . ."

At least she'd stepped in to stop Meadows having the last flicker of life kicked out of him. But probably that had been prudence rather than kindness. Rita must have known very well how tenacious the police get when one of their men has died.

The near-murder of Meadows had been enough to put the wind up her and her whole murdering brood. They'd hi-tailed it to the nearest hideout until the coast seemed clear, one of them probably staying in the neighbourhood to spy. And now they were back, gleefully scooping up the money they'd killed and maimed for, and probably chortling at the thought of what mugs the police in general and Matt Honiwell in particular, had been.

"There's fifty-seven thou in this sack now, as far as I can reckon it," one of the boys was saying.

"And forty-eight in this," came the girl's voice. "That's over a hundred thou. Can't we settle for that and get the hell out of here? This wind is bloody near killing me."

"And I'll be bloody near killing you if I hear any more talk like that!" yelled Rita. "There's the best part of two hundred thou still in that f-----g globe somewhere, just for the taking! Give it a kick, one of you, can't you? Or get a crowbar or summat to widen the split.''

There followed a deafening clanging and bashing, and the whole globe shuddered under the combined assaults of the family.

A second later, three things happened, almost simultaneously.

The tormented globe split right down the centre, the two halves falling apart and landing on the concrete with crashes that shook the whole forecourt. Notes, literally by the hundred thousand, blew everywhere, brushing against faces, hands, clothes, filling the darkness like a cloud of fluttering bats. And through the gloom, by the light of that one sixty-watt bulb, Matt could see Taffy Davis, with Drake and Foster alongside him, stealing up behind the Haigs. They were only about twenty yards away from them, but were proceeding with great difficulty, battling against the surrealistic blizzard of notes, which the wind was driving straight up into their faces.

Their approach, at all events, was entirely unnoticed by their quarry. Maddened by the sight of their disappearing loot, the Haigs were wholly occupied in chasing the notes, grabbing armfuls of them and clawing them down into the sacks which they were carrying.

Matt waited until Taffy and the others were only nine or ten yards behind the Haigs; then he produced his own revolver, and called out: "Right. You're under arrest, all of you. And we've got the drop on you, so you'd better come quietly — "

Never had the familiar police entreaty fallen on deafer ears.

Before Matt could finish the sentence, Rita was screaming: "It's Honiwell. Get him, kids. Don't forget, he's the bastard who done in your father."

The four Haig children dropped their sacks, and reached for their revolvers.

The sound of a mother calling on her children to kill left Matt so sickened that he momentarily forgot his own danger. He took a step forward, his voice shaking with fury as he shouted back: "*Did* I, Rita? *Did* I kill him — or *did you*?"

169

Obviously, the question hit home.

Rita's screaming rose to a hysterical pitch.

"Get him! Shut 'is rotten mouth, for God's sake! Shoot him, one of you, can't you – shoot to KILL – "

Shots rang out on all sides.

Bullets whizzed right and left of Matt, one thwacking into the brick wall behind him, two pinging into the remains of the bisected globe. Matt himself fired twice, to frighten rather than to kill. One of his shots was aimed about a foot to the left of Rita's body, the other just above the heads of the kids. The bullet aimed Rita's way whanged into a petrol pump just behind her. The other hit the windscreen of a used Cortina, and shattered glass fragments sprayed into the path of the three advancing policemen, who all had their revolvers out now, and were firing too.

"Right, you bastards, whatever you get, kindly remember you f------ asked for it!" roared Taffy Davis, blasting off three shots in the general direction of the Haigs.

Like Matt, he undoubtedly intended to fire wide. But a splinter of glass from the shattered windscreen hit him on his right cheek, just when he was pressing the trigger the first time. A banknote swept over his eyes and momentarily blinded him, the second time. And a shot from the eldest Haig boy, Richard, caught him in the right shoulder, so that the last bullet wasn't aimed at all, but was loosed accidentally from a revolver actually spinning out of his hand.

Ironically, it was this last, totally uncontrolled shot that ended the battle.

It hit Rita Haig high in her left thigh, only an inch or so below the hip. Her screams turned to an awful, hollow groaning and she dropped to her knees, blood pouring everywhere, especially over the notes that were still fluttering around her.

Blood money in name and fact, Matt thought grimly, as he moved in to make the arrests, a task that was accomplished surprisingly easily. There was no fight left in the Haig children now. Their only concern was that an ambulance should be fetched as rapidly as possible for their mother.

170

Decent, devoted kids, thought Matt, with sadness rather than irony. He wished he could share their concern for the woman who had turned them – as their own father had put it – into "bloody murdering gits".

* * *

Ten minutes later, the Haig children had been packed back into their estate car, and driven off to Aldgate Pump police station, with Foster at the wheel and a ferocious-looking Drake beside him, levelling a revolver over the back of his seat at his four prisoners. In a sense, the number had swollen to six. The two youngest Haig children, the fourteen-year-old Liz and twelve-year-old Barb, had been discovered crouching on the back seat, watching everything that was happening. They remained crouching there at the back all through the drive to the station, pale and silent once they had learnt the news about their mother.

Honiwell had not liked sending such a dangerous family to the station in the care of two inexperienced constables, but Davis's wound put him out of action, and he felt that he himself should sit with Rita, the key figure in the whole case, until the ambulance arrived.

In any event, he had taken the precaution of handcuffing the four eldest Haig children, and Drake and Foster, now that they had triumphantly survived their first shoot-out, were ten times the men they were before.

"So confident and pleased with themselves they are," Taffy Davis murmured, "that one would imagine they'd beaten the whole gang single-handed in a duel scene straight out of *High Noon*."

He winced as Matt tightened a hurriedly-made bandage round his shoulder.

"Very kind of you to bother, sir. But it's only a flesh wound, nothing to worry about. It's the lady who's in a bad way."

Matt had already made Rita as comfortable as he could, putting his own overcoat round her. But she was obviously still in pain, and giving long, low groans.

171

Matt walked over to her.

"Take it as easy as you can, Rita," he said, gently. "The ambulance will be here any minute."

"Come closer, Mr. Honiwell," Rita breathed. "There's something I've got to tell you. Kind of private, see . . ."

Matt dropped down on one knee beside her — and realised that, for what seemed the thousandth time, this woman had hoodwinked him, led him into a trap.

She had been so obviously sick that no one had troubled to search her; and now, from somewhere, she had produced a tiny, but very lethal-looking revolver, which she was levelling directly at his heart.

"For Lenny's sake, Honiwell, and for that f-----g lie you told about me killing him — "

She tried to squeeze the trigger, but weakness overcame her, and she almost fainted, giving Matt the chance he needed to snatch the gun away. Fear made him rougher than he'd intended to be. Rita yelped with agony, and he instantly earned the sneering gibe: "All right, I'm beaten, copper. There's no need to do a bleeding Riddell . . ."

*   *   *

Even as she said that, fifteen miles away in Kingston, Tom Riddell was making his crazy — almost literally crazy — bid to make sure that no one used his name like that again.

20 Riddell

For most of the six hours that had passed since he had left Sir Richard Ainley's flat in Mayfair, Tom Riddell had been wandering around London in a weird mental condition, one minute realising who he was and exactly what he had to do, and the next lost in a haze of doubt and indecision, all thought drowned by that buzzing in his head.

Over and over again he had to rebrief himself, saying, each time more sternly and decisively: *"You are Chief Detective Superintendent Riddell. You have discovered the hiding-place of Sid Stannet. You are on the way to arrest him for fifteen different offences, namely . . ."*

Sometimes he succeeded in remembering five of the offences, sometimes as many as ten. Then suddenly, at about eleven thirty in the evening, something clicked somewhere deep in his brain. He found that he could effortlessly remember all fifteen. He also remembered that he had no evidence against Stannet on any of these counts; that he had to carry out a super-bluff and break his nerve. But with the flash of mental clarity came a surge of confidence. If that was what he had to do, somehow he'd find a way to do it. And somewhere at the back of his mind, he already knew a way . . .

What was he waiting for? Why was he hanging about, walking up and down? Where the hell was he? It looked like the pavement of Piccadilly, outside Green Park. Yes, that was it. In the distance he could see the outline of the Ritz: over there was the entrance to Green Park Underground. He had to pull himself together, and get on that Underground. *Quickly.* Before that deafening, blinding buzzing in his head came back again . . . But it didn't come back again.

All the way to Kingston – by Underground to Waterloo via the Embankment, then out on the last suburban train – Riddell found his mind becoming clearer and clearer.

He was even able to analyse what had happened to him.

He had been on the brink of a breakdown, but was all right now.

And had a score to settle with the man who had brought him to that brink: Sid Stannet.

Stannet's pink, plump features seemed to swim in front of his eyes as he stepped out of Kingston station, and hailed a taxi.

The driver looked at him oddly at first, no doubt because of his wild appearance; but the man turned polite and respectful as Riddell said, in a tone of crisp command:

"The Gables. As fast as you can, please. I'm a police officer."

Kingston and its environs, from a silent but brightly-lit Bentalls to a rough and windswept Thames, flew past in a blur; and suddenly he was paying off the driver and knocking at the front door of a mansion-sized villa surrounded by acres of firs and pines, their branches swaying and lurching in the roaring wind. The door opened. Three vicious-looking henchmen appeared, dragged him into a mock-Tudor hall, frisked him and whipped away his revolver, all without saying a word.

Then a fourth henchman, a heavily-built thug who seemed comically anxious to sound like a butler, appeared and asked: "Would you kindly step this way please? Mr. Stannet is expecting you."

Riddell found himself being escorted into a vast, luxurious lounge, and suddenly, there in reality was that pink blancmange of a face he had seen so often in his mind's eye.

It was redder and shinier than he remembered it, suggesting that Stannet had been drinking a lot. And sweating a lot, too. There was no mistaking the uneasiness in those once-piercing,

174

but now pig-like eyes; an uneasiness that could rapidly be turned to fear, panic, terror if he played his cards right, Riddell thought.

And — his mind as clear as it had ever been — he felt suddenly certain that he was not going to play one wrong.

"Sidney Leon Vincent Stannet," he said very slowly and distinctly. "I am here to place you under arrest."

For a second, Stannet was too taken aback to speak. Then he recovered himself, and burst out laughing.

"Thomas Whatever-it-is Riddell," he said, mimicking the other's manner. "I've news for you. You're never going to place me, or anyone else, under arrest again. And do you know why? Because you're a washed-up copper, and a nutcase as well."

Riddell totally, even majestically, ignored the interruption.

"You are charged with the following offences," he continued, and in the same relentlessly slow, distinct voice, he recited all fifteen counts of the indictment on which Stannet had just stood trial.

As Stannet listened to the recitation, he had the uncomfortable feeling that he was back at the Old Bailey. He tried to laugh it off; to remind himself that he'd been acquitted of all these charges, and that under law, there was no way he could be tried for them again. But something about that relentless voice . . .

"Stop it, will you?" he snarled, as Riddell neared the end of his spiel. "I've been found *Not Guilty* on every one of those bloody charges, and if you don't remember that, you're even nuttier than I took you for."

"You were found not guilty, yes," Riddell said softly. There was something almost eerie about his total calmness as he added: "By a jury misled by wholesale perjury, in a trial that will be nullified when the Court of Appeal sees *these*."

He whipped out of his breast pocket a sheaf of closely-typed sheets of headed notepaper, which, in one of his moments of clarity, he had taken from a bureau in Sir Richard Ainley's library. The barrister had been facing a bookcase, with his hands in the air, at the time.

175

Riddell held the notepaper extremely carefully, so that Stannet could recognise Ainley's official heading, but not read a word of the typing. All he was really holding up was an assortment of letters selected completely at random. The top one sincerely regretted that Sir Richard would not be free to open a Christmas charity bazaar, but announced that a donation of £25 was enclosed herewith.

Stannet, though, was in such an inebriated state that he would have been unable to read the letters even if they had been held under his nose, let alone waved at him from across the room.

His face rapidly resembling a white rather than a pink blancmange, he staggered to the drinks cabinet and poured himself the fourteenth double whisky of the night.

"What the hell are those supposed to be?"

"Parts of a secret correspondence between Ainley and your solicitor, Casey-Barnes," Riddell announced, gravely, "which came to light when I broke into Ainley's flat and searched it, while I was waiting for him to come home this afternoon."

Stannet almost gulped down his whiskey. He knew about Riddell's hold-up of Ainley, of course. The barrister hadn't mentioned that the flat had already been broken into, but perhaps Riddell had been careful to leave few traces. The worrying thing was that what Riddell was saying *could* be true. Those documents *could* be real . . . "I found them very interesting reading, I assure you," Riddell went on mercilessly. "One letter, for instance, gives precise details of £20,000 worth of *ex gratia* payments – in other words, bribes – paid to key witnesses." He pretended to read from the sheets. "To 'Nosey' Knowles – £5,000. So that's what 'Nosey' got for saying that *I* had slipped him a thousand. To Ned Morris – £7,000. Ned earned his money, didn't he. He had himself beaten up so that he could claim *I* had done it to him during an interrogation. To Slim O'Casey – £4,000. That was for saying I'd employed him to forge documents – "

All these figures were completely spurious, but Riddell was counting on Stannet having left the actual sums either to Ainley or his crooked solicitor. And apparently he was right.

Stannet was shaking so much that he was now beyond the simplest action. Reaching for the whisky bottle, he upset half a dozen glasses. Two fell off the cabinet onto the deep-pile carpet. They did not break and made only the faintest tinkle. The sound was enough, though, to make Stannet start so violently that he nearly dropped the bottle.

"That fool Ainley," he said thickly. "I told – told him he should never keep records. In any case, the man's a twister, and so's – so's Casey-Barnes. I gave them £50,000, not £20,000 – " Suddenly a faint, flickering memory came to him that there were policemen hiding behind the curtain, and he finished hastily: " – towards the general expenses of the case, that is, of course."

"I wouldn't say you'd been done," Riddell said icily. "In fact, I'd call 'Not Guilty' on fifteen counts very cheap at the price." He put the sheaf of papers back in his breast pocket and folded his arms. "By the way, I hope you're not thinking of getting your henchmen to take these exhibits off me. There are photocopying agencies all over London, and I've been using one to good purpose today. If I'm not heard from by tomorrow, copies of the documents will be posted to the Public Prosecutor, the Home Secretary, and the Commissioner of Scotland Yard. So don't think you've finished with the Old Bailey, Stannet. Anytime now, they'll be hanging out the flags to welcome you back."

Stannet had to clutch hold of a corner of the drinks cabinet to stay on his feet. He had completely forgotten the hidden audience by now. All he could see or think about was Riddell, the policeman he had beaten, reviled, reduced to a nervous wreck, but who now seemed to be towering over him, the greatest danger he had faced in his entire career.

"If – if you've not heard from me by tomorrow?" he said. "That sounds as if you were trying – trying to do a deal with me. What do you want now, you lous – lousy copper, a Stannet handout yourself?"

"All I want is a signed confession, Sid," said Riddell levelly. "In return, I'll give you twenty-four hours to close down your rackets and quit the country. It's not an ideal arrangement from

177

my point of view. It's my job to leave slugs like you behind bars, not sunning themselves in some South American tax haven. But London will be a cleaner place without you, and that's something to be thankful — "

He broke off abruptly, as Stannet whipped out a revolver.

He hadn't expected that. He had thought that the threat of those incriminating photocopies going off in the post would have kept him safe.

Had he overplayed his hand?

His heart started thumping, and at each beat there was a stabbing pain behind his temples.

God, if that buzzing came back, he was sunk.

"Signed confession my ----," Stannet was saying crudely. His voice was suddenly soft and menacing. "Those copies haven't been posted yet, and they never will be posted, will they, once you're kind enough to tell me who's got them and who's sending them."

It was Riddell's turn to feel like swaying. But outwardly, he remained calm and even commanding.

"There's no way you can make me do that, Sid, and you know it."

Sid stood back from the table. Anger, fear and drink had combined to turn his cheeks back from white to a flaming red. His black eyes were as openly threatening as the muzzle of his revolver.

"There are hundreds of ways, and my lads know — know all of them," he said, and suddenly shouted out: "Boys, grab him!"

But it wasn't "the boys" who came in response to that command.

And it wasn't Riddell who was grabbed.

Alec Hobbs, with a stern-faced Stephenson and a jubilant Rance at his elbow, stepped out from behind the curtain and advanced on Stannet. Stephenson took one of his arms and Rance the other. Hobbs quietly relieved him of his gun.

"I think we've heard everything we need to know," murmured Alec smoothly. "And it seems to leave only one thing to be said. Sidney Leon Vincent Stannet, you are under arrest . . ."

178

An odd muttering sound from across the room made him look up.

Riddell, pale and swaying, was standing there with his eyes closed, talking softly to himself.

For the last time, that buzzing was filling his head; and for the last time, he was compelled to re-brief himself on the situation.

"You are Chief Detective Superintendent Riddell," he was whispering. "And – I think you're in the clear."

＊　　＊　　＊

A minute later, while his henchmen stood and watched in helpless disbelief, Sid Stannet was taken out of the house and into a police car.

Rance walked on one side of him, Stephenson on the other; Hobbs went in front, and Riddell, his mind already clear again, brought up the rear.

It was an arrest without precedent in Metropolitan police history. Stephenson and Rance were officially there as A10 Branch observers, and should not have been participating in the case at all. Hobbs was there on a kind of watching brief, under orders from Gideon to let Riddell have one last chance to prove that he was still a policeman. And Riddell himself was there under orders from his own partly clouded, partly brilliantly-functioning brain. Yet so skilfully had Sid Stannet been goaded into showing himself up as a vicious racketeer, that the four Yard men had instinctively closed ranks, and become simply coppers doing their duty.

In the charge room at Kingston police station, after Stannet had been led away to the cells, Bob Stephenson felt he had another duty to fulfil.

Solemnly, the man from Uniform, the lifelong hater of the C.I.D., walked up to Riddell and held out his hand.

In his oddly formal, witness-box style, he said: "At A10, we are under strict instructions never to let the subject of an inquiry know what will be in our report. But tonight I feel compelled to make an exception, Riddell. I cannot resist telling you that the way you dealt with Stannet was the cleverest and most courageous piece of police work I have witnessed in many, many years."

The stern side of Stephenson evidently told him not to be over-effusive.

"There were some irregularities, of course, and these will also be duly stressed. But considering the intense provocation to which you were subjected, and your uncertain state of health – "

He broke off, confused, and seemed grateful when Jimmy Rance came across, and butted in.

"What Stephenson and I are trying to say, Tom, is that you have nothing whatever to fear from A10. We thought it would make your mind easier if we told you so straightaway." His babyish face broke into a broad grin. "So please accept our congratulations – before you get the bill for what you did to our car last night."

Riddell was so shaken that for a moment he could hardly speak. Then, suddenly, he, too, was smiling.

"Thank you both – more than I can ever say. And thank you, too, for saving my skin. If you hadn't stepped out from behind that curtain at exactly that moment . . ." He stopped, frowning. "Incidentally, whose idea was it that you should stay in hiding and watch me in action, the way you did?"

"Do really need to ask?" Jimmy Rance said. "It was George, of course. He's the man you really want to thank, Tom. To be honest, he's the only one who's believed in you and kept fighting for you all through. Even against Scott-Marle."

Riddell ran a hand through his thick but greying hair.

"I certainly will thank him," he said. "Right away." He walked across the charge room to a phone, which stood on a plain wooden counter. "Hope I won't be getting him out of bed. I wonder if Kate Gideon's still round with Vi."

He was suddenly feeling awed and humble at the realisation of how much trouble he'd caused the Gideons, and how much he owed them. Surely no other police force in the world had a Commander who would care so deeply, and go to such infinite pains, over one – rogue cop!

He picked up the phone, but before he could start to dial, Alec

180

Hobbs came rushing in, a tense, strained Hobbs who had suddenly discovered that while they had been concentrating on the Stannet case, the greatest London emergency since the blitzes had been building up all round them.

Dante – the real Dante – was at large, heavily armed with incendiary grenades, he announced. Every patrol and area car had been commandeered to search for him. And at the heart of the crisis was the fact that the fire-brigade strike had been on for half an hour.

"Is Dante likely to be in this area?" asked Riddell.

"Very likely indeed," said Alec grimly. "And I'll tell you the likeliest place of all: Morden, about six miles south-east of here."

"Why Morden?"

"No logical reason. It's just that that happens to be where George has gone, and knowing George's uncanny habit of being in the right place at the right – "

A flash, bright as lightning but lasting three times as long, suddenly lit up the charge room's uncurtained window; and as the four men rushed towards it, a roar, like a dozen thunderclaps rolled into one, shook the whole building.

By the time they reached the window, a vivid red glow was already colouring about a third of the sky, directly ahead.

"Which way does this window face?" Hobbs asked a uniformed sergeant, behind the counter.

The sergeant, himself shaken, nevertheless answered promptly.

"South, sir. To be exact, south-south-east. You're looking directly towards Morden."

181

21 Inferno

Never in his career had an event taken Gideon so completely by surprise.

He was lying in the patch of gorse scrubland, having just pulled Timothy Dane alongside him, and together they were watching the approach of the small Citroën. In the softest of whispers, he was telling Dane: "If my reasoning is right, he'll come alongside here and turn the car, in readiness for a quick getaway. After that, he'll get out and try to lob one, perhaps two, of those glass bombs over the fence. That will be my big chance to act."

"Chance?" said Dane, equally softly. "What sort of chance will you have against a man armed with a firestorm?"

"That's my problem," Gideon said. "Yours is simply to get yourself as far away from here, as fast as you can. Take off now. Keep your head down. Keep running. And good luck."

The Citroën was now about twenty yards away. It was still entirely without lights, but at this distance, it was just possible to make out the tall figure of Cabot, hunched tensely behind the wheel. He slowed down to walking pace, and was peering intently right, in the direction of the tank complex. Probably he was already judging the best angle at which to throw his first incendiary globe.

"Quick," Gideon urged Dane. "He's not looking this way. Now's your opportunity."

"Now," said Dane, in his oddly pedantic voice, "is my

opportunity indeed.''

To Gideon's horror and amazement, he suddenly rose to his full height, and began to run towards the car.

Gideon leaped after him, caught him by the right arm — and then let go of him faster than he had ever released anybody in his life.

He had glimpsed a gleaming object in Dane's hand — glassy, round, about the size of a cricket ball . . .

He remembered that he had left Dane alone upstairs at Cabot's home for minutes while he had talked to Scott-Marle on the phone. Obviously he had gone back to the laboratory and pocketed one of the globes. But — why?

Shakily, he asked the question aloud.

''Why?''

Dane turned back for just two seconds, and answered in just three sentences.

''It's very simple, Commander. He made fires follow me everywhere. Now my fire is going to follow him.''

He swung round, and started running again, straight down the mud track towards the Citroën, which was proceeding at walking pace, barely six yards away. Cabot was still peering right, towards the tank complex, and was so intent on his schemes for the night ahead that he neither heard nor saw Dane approach the car.

The first thing he knew about it was when the front left-hand door was swung open, and an object was flung in to fall and break at his feet with a glassy tinkle.

Cabot needed no telling what that object was. There were thirty just like it on the back seat behind him — carefully laid out in rows, packed between wadding. Nor did he need any telling what happened two to three seconds after one was broken . . .

In a sudden wild panic, he brought the car to a juddering halt, and grabbed at the handle of the right-hand door. But his hands were sweaty and fumbling, and it took him a second, a very, very precious second, to get the door open.

And before he could move from his seat, he had company.

Someone — someone absurdly light and frail, but powered by

183

an almost demonic fury – hurled himself into the car, and seized him by the throat. Even in the gloom, and even through the red mist of hysteria, Cabot made out the matted beard and staring eyes of his dim, alcoholic dupe, Timothy Dane.

"Dane!" he choked out. "Are you completely mad?"

"No madder than you made me," said Dane, and maintained his ferocious grip on Cabot until the last precious second had flashed by.

And Dante was in his inferno.

*   *   *

Gideon, standing about twelve yards further back along the mud track, saw the entire front half of the Citroën vanish in a single, searing flash.

In the nick of time, he remembered what was, in all probability, in the rear half, and dropped flat on his face.

The next instant, the very ground on which he landed seemed to shudder as, with a roar, the rest of the Citroën simply blew apart.

Bits of molten metal whanged past, inches above Gideon's head. And when he cautiously peered in the direction of where the car had been, a strangely Biblical spectacle met his eyes: for a moment, a blood-red pillar of fire reared thirty, forty, fifty feet above him, bathing everything – the factory fence, the grass, the trees, his own clothing – in an unearthly crimson light. Then, fast as a bubble bursting, the pillar vanished and the roar of air being sucked into the vacuum was like the rumbling of a dozen volcanoes.

And in the wake of that rumbling came a new horror, unlike anything Gideon had ever experienced.

Quite suddenly, without the slightest warning, he found that there was no air to breathe.

His senses swam. His lungs felt like bursting. Blind panic threatened to paralyse every limb. But deep in its centre, his brain remained calm, telling him that this was the firestorm effect that Dane had talked about; that it must be strictly localised; that if he could run far enough, fast enough –

Somehow he forced himself to get to his feet, and ran stumbl-ingly across the scrubland away from where the Citroën had been.

After about thirty yards, his bursting lungs could not sustain the effort any longer, and he fell forward on his knees, his gasps getting weaker and weaker, until suddenly some kind of miracle happened, and they turned into *gulps*.

Gulps of bitter, frosty – but very, very welcome – November air.

After just a few of them, Gideon scrambled to his feet, only to be knocked flat on his back by a bigger flash, a still more deafening roar.

The tank complex had caught alight, he realised. In seconds, the whole factory would be blazing. And, if the Green God-desses couldn't cope, within minutes, the whole of Morden.

Had Cabot won in spite of everything? Was this the start of a Great Fire of London after all?

Gideon realised that he was now only yards away from his partially-hidden Rover. He decided to make for it. At least, the radio in there could tell him what was going on, why there were no police cars, no fire-engines –

He had just reached the Rover when he heard what at first he took to be a ringing in his ears.

Then he realised it was the distant clanging of a fire-engine bell, accompaned by wailing sirens.

He rushed back towards the mud track, recklessly ignoring the roars and explosions from the other side of the factory fence, and was in time to see the first of the fire-engines arrive.

At the sight of it, his heart started racing, not with excitement, but with sheer relief.

It was a regular fire-brigade engine, which meant that somehow, and for some reason, the strike had been halted.

London was safe at last.

*   *   *

Half an hour later – by which time, the fire had already been brought largely under control – the fire-brigade chief took Gideon aside, and told him: "It's just the Wimbledon firemen who are back, sir, the ones who'd worked under Cabot. Quite frankly, hero or not, he was the biggest bastard we've ever had in the brigade. And when the news came over the radio that *he* was the real Dante – well, the men couldn't get back fast enough to stop his little game. The Union may blackball them all in the morning, but somehow I don't think they will."

Gideon's reply was held up by the roar of yet another part of the factory collapsing in smoke and flame. But it was followed immediately by a reassuring hissing, and clouds of steam testified to the efficiency with which the sweating firemen were combating the blaze.

"I don't think they will either," Gideon said at length. "After all, they're all Londoners in the Union, aren't they? And London is what you're rescuing."

The fire-brigade chief frowned.

"All the same, the boys will probably be had up before the Union's branch committee and fined," he said.

Then, suddenly, he grinned and reluctantly conceded: "But they'll probably feel that it's almost a pleasure to pay."

Gideon laughed, and walked away, back to his Rover. He got in it, switched on the radio, and gave a full account of all that had happened, first to Scotland Yard, then to the Chief Inspector at Wimbledon. This done, he sat for a moment silently behind the wheel.

The last time he had sat here, Timothy Dane had been beside him.

He could never forget that what had really stopped London becoming a vast Dante inferno was the quixotic gallantry of this despised drop-out.

It was entirely possible that he owed him his own life.

Which made the thought of all that had been done to Dane suddenly quite unbearable. He had been wrongfully arrested, brutally beaten-up. A spurious confession had been wrung from him. He had been hounded by 7,000 men across the whole Wimbledon area, and finally re-arrested on a wholly trumped-up charge.

If he, Gideon, hadn't personally intervened, Farrant would almost certainly have beaten Dane up again, and the evidence of that powder planted on his coat could have ensured him a jail sentence for life.

Quite clearly, he owed it to Dane's memory to make sure that John Farrant could never behave like this to anyone again. The trouble was that he still hadn't positive proof of Farrant's guilt. Dane had been in Cabot's house, where the laboratory was full of the Dante powder. Some of it *could* have strayed on to his coat, and Farrant's find could have been perfectly genuine.

Gideon sighed. It seemed as if he was fated to give Farrant the benefit of the doubt for ever.

He swung the Rover round, and, avoiding the mud track (where the remains of the holocaust would have to be examined by police experts) drove it across the scrubland towards the road. As he neared it, a chaotic scene met his eye. Police cars had now arrived by the dozen, and were filling, and blocking, the road. In the midst of them, men from the B.B.C. and I.T.V. newsvans were desperately trying to set up their equipment in time to capture the last of the blaze that could have been the beginning of the end of London.

There was no possibility of driving anywhere until this mess was sorted out, thought Gideon. He stopped the car on the edge of the patch of scrubland and scrambled out.

At just that moment, a familiar figure emerged from the nearest of the police cars and came towards him.

"Very glad to see that you're all right, sir," said Farrant, as brightly and eagerly as ever. "I hear from Wimbledon that Dante's had it. Gone up in a kind of firestorm . . ."

He seemed to have no awareness of the fact that by his criminal mishandling of the case, he had endangered the whole of London.

Gideon nodded.

"Very dangerous, these Dante chemicals," he said, almost chattily. "Just half a teaspoonful of that powder, for instance, if jolted accidentally, or too hurriedly exposed to the air, would create an instant holocaust."

187

He was making these facts up as he went along. But he thought Farrant might find them interesting, particularly if he still had any quantity of the stuff on him. He would be unlikely to have unloaded every speck on to Timothy Dane's suit . . .

Farrant started violently, and his right hand flew to his breast pocket. Before it could reach it, Gideon's hand had closed over Farrant's fist.

"Just pull out what you've got in there," Gideon said softly. Farrant stared.

"Really, sir. I – I think you're over-reaching yourself."

"Never mind about what I'm doing. Just you reach into that pocket," Gideon roared.

Farrant realised that he had no choice but to obey.

A crumpled envelope emerged, and in the red, flickering light from the dying blaze, Gideon could see that it contained a good teaspoonful of the grey Dante powder. Very much more than could be picked off any coat . . .

Farrant, for once, was confused and stammering.

"I was certain – we were all certain – that Dane was Dante. And there was – there was no other way to make sure the charge against him stuck," he muttered.

"No," said Gideon, very, very grimly. "There never is any other way for you, Farrant, is there, except the lying way, the cheating way, the bullying way. Your sort bring contempt on the whole C.I.D. So don't blame me if just for once I bring some down on you. You are suspended from this minute. And tomorrow this envelope goes straight to Macgregor of A10."

He turned on his heels and walked away.

Farrant made no attempt to call him back or argue. He knew it would not be the slightest use.

Under Gideon's Law, once there was no possibility of doubt, there was no possibility of mercy for any crooked cop.

188

22 Law

The death of Timothy Dane, the suspension of Farrant, the relentless tension of the past twenty-four hours – to say nothing of the scratches and bruises he had sustained during that frantic scramble over scrubland in search of air – had taken their toll of Gideon.

When, a few minutes later, he found himself surrounded by T.V. newsmen and asked to make a statement, it was almost beyond him to say anything sensible at all. He managed to express some sort of thanks for the way the whole police force had responded to the emergency, and to the Wimbledon fire brigade for having "put London first and Union problems second". Then he wondered dazedly if he was being too political, and escaped from the cameras before any more questions were asked at all.

There was nothing more he could usefully accomplish here tonight, he decided. There were not even any visible remains of Dane or Cabot to be guarded, or taken to the police mortuary. There was only a crater in the mud track with which the forensic experts would be having a field-day tomorrow. There would be time enough to deal with all the remaining problems then.

Tired, hungry and not far from nervous exhaustion, Gideon only just had the strength to battle his way through the crowd to his Rover, climb in, and head for home.

Once there, though, his spirits very rapidly revived.

Kate was waiting with lashings of hot, strong tea, and after

189

taking one look at him—"poor darling, you must be starving"—rushed off to the kitchen and cooked the lightest and most delicious cheese omelette he had ever tasted. Over the meal—served, as on all emergency occasions, at the kitchen table—she gave him the startling news that Sir Reginald Scott-Marle had just rung to offer Gideon his personal congratulations, and those of the Home Secretary, for so brilliantly dealing with the Dante menace.

Kate was also full of all that had happened at the Riddells'. She had been there with Vi when Tom had arrived back at the house, and had never seen such a moving homecoming. Tom had seemed completely his old self, Kate went on, and added, almost as an afterthought, that she believed Alec and the A10 men had *arrested* Sid Stannet.

"What?" said Gideon, and almost dropped his fork for joy.

Alec Hobbs himself rang up shortly afterwards—a very anxious Alec, who had been caught in the mêlée of police cars converging on Morden, and was not sure if Gideon was alive or dead. Once satisfied on that score, he was happy to give the full details of what had happened at the Stannet hideout.

"There's no doubt that Stannet faces a re-trial now, George, and he'll have his work cut out to twist the law round his little finger this time. It's more than likely we'll have Ainley and his solicitor crony Casey-Barnes up there in the dock beside him."

"All thanks to Tom, eh?" said Gideon.

"Very definitely, all thanks to Tom! How he could have brought it off in that confused mental state, and how you *knew* he could bring it off, I can't imagine."

Gideon chuckled.

"Nothing miraculous about it. Tom's a good cop. Always has been, always will be. And good cops just don't turn into bad ones overnight, no matter what the pressures may be."

This thesis was startlingly confirmed a minute later, when Matt Honiwell came on the line to report on the events at the Haig garage.

At the end of his story, he said wryly: "Funny when you come to think of it, George. There we were, four policemen up to our knees in banknotes, not merely ignoring them, but risking our lives to see that they didn't wind up in the wrong hands! And they say there are only crooks left in the C.I.D.!''

Gideon was feeling almost light-hearted when he put down the phone.

Tom Riddell's name had been cleared. Stannet and his bent legal aids were facing prosecution. The most murderous bank-robbers in recent history had been caught red-handed, barely forty-eight hours after their bloody snatch. Lenny Haig's death had been shown to have had nothing to do with Matt's questioning. The real Dante had been found, and stopped, before he could carry out any part of his apocalyptic threat to London. And the wrongs done to Timothy Dane had been, to some extent at least, avenged.

One thing, then, had emerged from this chaotic night stronger than it had been for months, perhaps years.

And it wasn't a little thing.

To Gideon it was, perhaps, the biggest thing of all.

The Law.